TEMPORIUM

TEMPORIUM

BEFORE THE BEGINNING TO AFTER THE END

FICTIONS

Kelly Cherry

Press 53
Winston-Salem

Press 53, LLC
PO Box 30314
Winston-Salem, NC 27130

First Edition

Cover design by Kevin Morgan Watson

Cover art, "Unsplash," by Josep Castells via Pexels

Author photo by Burke Davis III

Library of Congress Control Number 2017954775

Printed on acid-free paper
ISBN 978-1-941209-57-8 (softcover)
ISBN 978-1-941209-58-5 (hardcover)

This book is dedicated to my students of yore,
because *almost all* of them worked hard
and asked stimulating questions,
and some of them taught *me*.

Grateful thanks to the editors of the publications listed below for first publishing the following stories:

American Letters and Commentary, "Municipal" (as "Civic Lessons"), "Young Men of Prague" (reprinted in *Redux 2016*).
Arts and Letters, "Fugue"
Blue Fifth Notebook, "Aquarium"
Boulevard, "Vasily Vasilyevich Sliwowitz"
Commentary Magazine, "The Train"
The Cortland Review, "Saturday's Child"
Gargoyle, "God: A Prolegomenon," "A Dream with the Wind in It"
Hotel Amerika, "Beginning as Other," "The End of Time"
Idaho Review, "Speaking Vanish"
Jeopardy, "Agenda"
Kentucky Review, "Abebe"
Lake City Lights, "The Door Bell," "Nostalgia of the Infinite"
Monkeybicycle, "Another Collective Noun for 'Quail,'" "Looking for Love," and "Defining the Indefinable"
New Flash Fiction Review, "Seniors at the Movie"
North American Review, "Eternity Dies"
NumeroCinq Magazine, "On Teaching," "Burning the Baby," "Derek," and "Drought"
Peacock Journal, "Murray, the Short Order Cook" and "Aegea"
Per Contra, "Diana Awaiting Her Death in the Colosseum," "Liling"
Potomac, "How She's Changed"
Punctuate!, "Six Words (Dead Husband)," "Five Words (Woman Exeunt)"
Shenandoah, "Reunion"

Anthologies
"Abebe," *The Kentucky Review Anthology, 2016*
"The Department of Mirth and Laughter," *Flash Fiction Funny*. ed. Hazuka and Thomas (Blue Light Press, 2013)
"A Dream with the Wind in It." *The Best Small Fictions 2105*, ed. by Robert Olen Butler and Tara Masih (Queen's Ferry Press, 2016)

Contents

This is something like, but not altogether like, a short-story collection, because not all of these pieces are stories. Nor is this a collection of prose poetry, though one or two entries may come close to that. At least a few of them are more like mini-essays, though perhaps they are not essays, either. What they are—these bits and pieces—is moments of time and I have arranged them more or less chronologically. I think of the book as a museum, curating, harboring, or displaying the moments collected herein. Hence the title.

KC

THE AGENDA

First on the agenda today is the topic of mystery. We have convened here to consider this majestic subject from all points of view that are available to us. Feel free to say whatever comes into your mind. You may doodle. Legal-sized writing tablets have been provided for doodling.

Is mystery more than ignorance? That is the topic. For example, is what we are facing here what we do not know, or what we cannot know, or something that refuses to be known?

A possible approach to this question may be from the southwest.

Here is our slide presentation: A small cloud in a fit of fury flings itself down from the Catalinas; it becomes mild, almost sweet-tempered; it dies in the desert, snagged on saguaro. Has the narrative of the cloud any bearing on our topic? Perhaps not. Has it any bearing on the wood duck, drifting downstream like driftwood, past a clump of cottonwood trees? Perhaps not.

Yes, a water glass has been provided for each of you, as well as ashtrays for those who persist in smoking.

Shall we continue? That is the second item on the agenda. Shall we continue? Shall we continue? You may say whatever comes into your mind. You may doodle.

GOD: A PROLEGOMENON

Start here: If God does not know time, he exists in a state of
ignorance. This particular state of ignorance, moreover, must
be eternal, it must lie outside time. A God who does not know
time would be, therefore, both ignorant and eternally ignorant.
And it is insupportable that we should have such a God, is it not,
since such a God would be, at best, useless, perhaps a nuisance,
and at worst dangerous. An ignorant God! A God who has never
known, does not know now, and never will know, time! That is
to say, us! Clearly, God must know time. But it is one thing to
say that God does know time and another to admit that God
must know time. If God must know time, he is bound by laws of
logic. He is not omnipotent. Tethered to the laws of logic, he is a
ninety-pound weakling, a God who cannot do everything, a
Walter Mitty of a God. That is to say, not God! How to resolve
this quandary? God, it seems, can choose to be less than
omniscient, or he can choose to surrender himself to logic. God
is free, then, although his freedom consists in choosing the precise
way in which he will not be what he is—namely, himself, God.
How else are we to account for famine in Africa, an earthquake
in Armenia or anywhere? We may say he is unkind, but that is to
say he is no God at all.—Unkind, he is a non-God, who, the very
moment a sparrow spins downward on a fatal feather of air,
carefully averts his gaze. Or have we, on the other hand, a God

who, not unkind, looks on the broken cities and starving people and loathes himself for being able to do nothing beyond whatever is logical, or even just tactical (as in relief aid, coordinated efforts)? But the answer is evident in psychology, if not philosophy: How could any God not be curious about his creation, not care whether it is, in his created world, spring or autumn, night or day. . . if the sun is wrapped in a shawl of clouds. . . or dancing in the sky. . . or that it is night, streets glistening in a fine mist, the skyline splashed, it almost seems, from an Evian bottle, the way models spritz their faces to keep their complexions looking youthful. . . ? As for Aristotle, who dares to disagree—to hell with him. Aristotle argues that the perfect cannot know the imperfect. The greater cannot know the lesser. To know imperfection is to partake of it. Thus Aristotle's God languishes in self-contemplation, an excess of self-contemplation, one might say, if that were not to beg the question, but even without begging it, we can see that this God of Aristotle's magnifies himself, becomes blimplike with narcissism, a desuetude that swells and ripens and overripens and decays, self-love decomposing into self-hatred, and what kind of God have you then, I ask Aristotle, what kind? A God not unlike a man, if you know what I mean. All swollen with self-importance, vain as all get-out, and then he starts to resent his own being for taking up so much room, for occupying his every thought, and this makes him angry with himself, and then he takes it out on everyone else. And this is another way to understand earthquakes, famine, and the countless forms of hurt that exist on our planet, whole species of hardship and sorrow yet to be identified and named. But Aristotle is wrong, as he was wrong when he classified woman as a lesser man (we, if we wanted to, could draw a line of inheritance from Aristotle through Aquinas to Freud). The perfect loves the imperfect. It loves the imperfect because it is imperfect, because it is not itself. That it does, that the perfect loves the imperfect, follows on the self-contradiction, noted above, inherent in the idea of the perfect loving the perfect. Ergo, God loves time because it is not himself. (Quod erat demonstrandum, and here we have it.) (By the way, is there a truer transcendence, a sweeter grace than that to be found in the act of adoration for what is not oneself? No.) He loves it, and thereby comes to know it. (Quod erat demonstrandum ditto—which is no joke.) Comes to know it in every detail, like obsession, or devotion: the stars' and seasons' passages, the creatures born and hurtling toward death. He loves all this the way he loves the great emptiness at the center of himself, the part of himself that he is not. For, remember, he has chosen not to be all that he is, and it is that absence in himself, that part of himself that he has relinquished, given up, sacrificed, that he loves and knows, that part of himself that is crucified and dying. And this is how it is that God has placed himself in thrall to time and all its laws, forever, even though great anxiety now bedevils him always, the anxiety of the lover. Who is anxious on behalf of the beloved, helpless—with speeding heart, held breath—oh! doomed, doomed to allow the beloved to live apart from him, die apart too. The anxiety of the lover who is terrified and wanting to be loved, even as he forsakes love for the sake of love. And this is why, this is why he is calling to us, even now, our names echoing down through the amaranthine corridor of centuries

ETERNITY DIES

Eternity is in love with the productions of time.
—William Blake, *Proverbs of Hell*

There was no knowing how long he had waited, nor had he known even that he was waiting, because duration and anticipation were not yet ideas he had thought of. Oh, he knew all there was to know; he was omniscient, after all. But he *was* all there was to know. He did not yet know all that there could or would be to know. The ideas of "yet" and "not yet" remained unthought.

He lived in a world of unimaginable—to us—density, because he was the whole of that world. He was all solid radiance, possibility itself packed to the mathematical point of first existence, a density nothing actual can equal since, of course, that was coterminously the omega-point of first non-existence. His temperature measured in the trillions of degrees. He was on fire, burning with knowledge; he was brilliant. Yet because he was All, and contained All, and there was nothing that was not already known to him because there was nothing that was not contained in him, he was lonely, and he had been lonely for longer than he could know.

Feverish, and lonely.

And it was that—his reflecting that he was lonely—which brought the universe into being. He thought to himself, I am lonely—and everything that is came into being, or at least the beginning of it did. It was separate from him, and in this separation, the simple fact of separation, dwelled hope—this was the First Hope—hope of reunion; at the same time, that which was separate from him was necessarily forever-separate, if that hope were not to be extinguished. He had thought this thought: I am lonely, and the universe exploded into existence, a fireball so intense it was white, with a whiteness never again to be equaled. Light and energy poured from him; he felt the shock of that transmission. Good, he thought; it was good. But he despaired of ever being whole again. That was the First Despair. It was he who had brought despair into being, by becoming his nonself.

Let us proceed from here: We have calculated that at 10^{-43} seconds after his thinking, I am lonely, his density was only 10^{90} tons per cubic inch. Dense almost beyond belief, this was nevertheless a finite density.

At the age of one second, the universe had a density that was the density of water, and as the universe expanded, the energy released condensed into matter and antimatter: electrons, protons, neutrons, hydrogen and helium.

All this followed logically on the thought of his loneliness. His thinking that thought was the First Cause. Thus even the First Cause was caused, but it was also uncaused, because it was not caused by anything that existed. It was caused before existence existed, by his thinking of his loneliness.

All this happened in about three minutes, and then a million years elapsed, until the temperature of the universe had cooled enough for atoms to form. Atoms permitted the light to travel through them; accordingly, the universe became visible.

He was despairing, and full of hope, and learning time, watching the universe take shape. He thought of duration, of anticipation. These were ideas entailed by the logic of despair and hope, and so it was logical that he should think of them, despairing and hoping, and all the while, he was watching the universe take shape.

The light and energy that were radiating from him were moving outward, farther and farther, spreading like water. Clouds of hydrogen cartwheeled through space. Like partners in a random celebration, a cosmic jubilee, atoms occasionally touched, and where they did so, small clumps of condensed gas burst into being. Where atoms came together in groups large enough to exert enough gravity, they cohered. Eventually, a cloud would collapse inward, the atoms' gravity tugging them toward the center, and the temperature at the cloud's center climbed. When the temperature reached 20 million degrees Fahrenheit, and the diameter was a mere one million miles, the ball became a fireball. This nuclear fire liberated the energy that had been locked inside; the energy radiated light and heat, as he did. Stars. He was the Star of stars.

The burning up of the hydrogen resulted in "ashes" of new elements. The materials of our universe are byproducts. The first element, hydrogen, had been the byproduct, or residue, of a thought, the thought of his loneliness. He had created, from the beginning, in his own image.

There was no other way.

And now there were galaxies and stars, and some light and energy lessened, loosened, as the hydrogen converted itself into heavier elements, and now there were solar systems, including our own.

When the planets had formed out of bits of rock and shimmering crystals of ice slowly orbiting the new sun, ours began to melt at the core, where the radioactive atoms were disintegrating. Volcanos were spawned. Lava flowed over the hard rock surface of the earth, carrying sulphurous gas that condensed into water. Oceans rained.

Methane drifted ominously over the chilly planet; the oceans were still one large ocean. Lightning fragmented the sky; the span of sky was like a puzzle whose pieces have been shaken from a box onto the cardtable; the pieces' edges were jagged, like combs with broken teeth, or a broken window. It was the beginning of life as we know it, this lightning; it mixed the atmospheric gases into new atomic arrangements known as amino acids.

Soon, then: molecules that reproduced themselves. DNA. Protozoa. The phyla, the species. And then: trees, mosses, salamanders, sharks, the woolly mammoth.

And riptides and continents, continental plates, and people and their stories about themselves, the long attempt to make sense beginning.

He watched all this activity that was separate from himself, and longing filled him as if he were a basin, and his desire, rain— rain that went on for whole eons. It seemed to him that only now did he know precisely how lonely he had been. That was the First Irony.

Fishes and dinosaurs! The glyptodont—the giant armadillo— and the saber-toothed tiger! Birds' wings fanning the tops of eucalyptus trees, and the platypus trundling around Australia, and the lemming throwing itself off a cliff, and elephants, and trillium, and tapestries woven by creatures that walked on two legs! How he longed to be one of these last, walking among them, sharing their meals, telling them—oh, yes!—telling them all that he had to say.

It was like being alone, this apartness, this separation. He was lonely—and indeed he felt as if he might as well still be alone. Everything had emanated from him, he had created the panorama in all its details and fineness, but his own generosity— Or was it selfishness? He thought it might be both at once—had isolated him. There was something leprous in him, he decided. Something self-consuming, and hideous to others.

And then, as he was gazing on the earth, tears in his eyes—but he refused to let them fall, yet—he saw. . . a thing. A thing in particular. He had to peer more closely, to squint, in fact—it was so small.

It was a potato vine, and it was growing in Peru.

There were very many wild potatoes then, in Peru and parts of Argentina and "on the coastal plains of southern Chile," and in Colombia, Bolivia, Ecuador. Some were red- or purple- or yellow-skinned, scabby-looking. They were round or oval or elliptical or oblong. They had deep eyes, and some could be said to "look like concertinas," according to J.G. Hawkes, and others like "worms or snakes." They were cultivated by Indians who lived around Lake Titicaca. Today, in the Mantaro Valley of Peru, there is a scientific collection of over 12,000 varieties of potato. The potato known as Chapiña is black, through and through; the natives used it to dye cloth.

It was Chapiña he saw, and now he saw the tiny tuber below the topsoil (he could, certainly, see everywhere, although some things were harder to see than others). He saw its thumb-sized black-through-and-through lumpy potato-body; and he fell in love.

Perhaps it was ridiculous: to fall in love with a potato. The world held so many things, live and inanimate, and even some, such as viruses, that were sometimes one and sometimes the other. But love is love; it occurs at first sight—when the proper seeds have been planted in the right soil, and the time is ripe—and so it was that he fell in love with a potato.

Such a little potato! Such a black potato! Such a Chapiña!

He had been so lonely and so alone for so long, and now he felt an urgency he had never before known. He felt a will to language.

He wanted—oh, so much!—to tell the potato of his love.

Cautiously, he bent his spirit toward Peru. Chapiña, under the earth, noticed nothing.

It was a clear day. The blue sky sang with mosquitoes and dragonflies; trees turned their leaves toward the sun; the peaks of the Andes sparkled as if stars were embedded in their snowbanks. Flamingos flew upward like flames, as if the air were on fire. Parrots gazed around philosophically; mountains rose on one side and sloped downward on the other, running to ground.

He bent his spirit; he touched earth.

"Chapiña," he whispered.

The little potato could not speak. (Did you think it could speak? It was a potato.)

He went down into the earth, as if entering a sepulchre in a garden. Chapiña looked at him, all those deep eyes staring at him through the darkness.

And then those eyes began to weep. He himself had not yet learned how to weep, but Chapiña knew how. The little Peruvian potato wept and wept.

"Don't cry," he said.

And now, miraculously, Chapiña could speak. Because it was not necessary for the potato actually to speak: He could hear everything the little potato thought.

How can I not cry, thought the little black potato, and he heard the words as if they had been spoken. Anyone would cry, in my place. You say you love me. Well, it's all right for you to love me, but how can I love you? I have nothing to give you in return, no arms to hold you with. You created me, but you forgot to make me capable of loving you. You never stopped to think how cruel you were being.

Of course this speech broke God's heart; he wondered if he had ever heard anything so sad as Chapiña's words. Why,

Chapiña was as sad as he had been back before there had been anything outside himself, when, being All, he had thought, I am lonely. And he was the cause of this other being's sadness.

He wept. Just as it says in the Bible, he wept.

He was filled with remorse and painful confusion, with guilt.

He wept, and the little potato, wanting to wipe his tears away, extended its tentacles, wrapping him in a warm embrace. Earth stopped up his mouth, his eyes; he was buried in earth. He was happy.

Yes, happy! It was not something he had ever thought of before, happiness, and it was something he recognized as soon as he perceived the possibility of redemption. To love Chapiña— to love anything or anyone like this was to triumph over Irony, and Despair, and even Hope. To love like this was to be companioned, embraced, chosen. To love like this was to be joined together, forever un-separate.

And so he died, his spirit nourishing the earth he had made. And the earth grew rich and complex, layered with new meaning, fertile with nuance. Everything else, that was to be, sprang into being when it was ready: paradox and implication, and resonance and consequence.

Thus did eternity depart from us, giving us time. And that is why, from that day to this, there has existed only time, and the memory of what we are rooted in.

SIX WORDS

Jesus Saves. First Bank of America.

DIANA AWAITING HER DEATH
IN THE COLOSSEUM

The body would be devoured and ravened by the lions just as she had satiated her appetite with fish from the Tiber, quail's eggs, pig. The creatures would dismember her. She would be pierced by fangs, torn, swallowed, taken in and absorbed. It was what it meant to be a body. It was only the body, not the spirit.

The stadium seats were crammed to capacity with a jostling crowd. Shouts, hoots, jeers, laughter. She noticed, among the thousands of spectators, a couple who appeared to be paying no attention to what was going on in the arena. They had their heads together as if small winds, blowing at their backs, pushed them into each other.

She noticed, too, that the sky was blue, unblemished by clouds. She tried to imagine the blueness as foundational, the ground floor of God's kingdom. If Christ could walk on water, a city could fly. There would be a room for her there, in his father's house. A small, private room with tile to walk on, cool as a pool to the bottoms of her bare feet and inlaid with a mosaic of semiprecious stones in the shape of fish, which was his sign. Fish from the Tiber.

A spray of blood brushed her cheek as softly as if someone had touched her face with a rose. Her father had tended the roses at home, coaxing them out of the hot ground.

She swiped at the thickish wetness with her hand, getting blood on her fingertips.

The crowd roared. Like a lion!

From the corner of her eye she could see the iron gates opening, more of the beasts, starved into rage, entering the arena. It was not God who had ordained death but humans, with their willfulness and lust to possess and accidental cravings.

She could not bring herself to look around for her parents, for their bodies, broken like bread.

Body was not spirit.

She had selected for herself a line of sight through which she could see the blue sky. And there was the young couple, so intent on each other, so engaged.

She could smell the blood; and it was slick on her fingertips, it was silken as rose petals. She could hear the screams and prayers, the agonized hollowness of them, as if they reached her from a distance, fogged and echoey with travel. Blue ribbons of screams.

There was such a heaviness to it all, as well: the huge animals, the human carcasses, the clapping and stomping in the stands. This mayhem, this circus. The stadium seemed to be shuddering.

She fitted her hands together to pray, and the hand with blood on it imprinted the other, and seeing her hands so clasped, she remembered her sister, Julia, who had died of fever so long ago that Diana wasn't always sure she had had a sister, except for the way they had held hands when they ran into the water on vacation. "Oh!" Julia cried, seeing the ocean for the first time at four. "It's full!"

She knelt, then, and began to pray, planning that the last words she would hear would be those of the Lord, who taught us to pray, "Our Father, which art in heaven." And so many others were there as well. Would Julia, she wondered, with red hair and pretty, smiling mouth open with pleasure—how vividly she remembered her little sister now—be there waiting for her? Would she see her parents there, later this afternoon? "Mother, Father," she would cry, leaping over stars to reach them, "I'm here too!" The thought of how happy they would be to see her made her start to cry. It was all she ever wanted: for them to be happy. Why was she crying? Was she not grateful to God for this gift he had conferred on her, this opportunity to please her parents? She smoothed the tears from her face with the heels of her hands.

Little quail egg, she said to herself, squeezing her eyes shut tight now, a blackness surrounding, descending, blue sky burnt to blackness, piglet, fishling. For you, such an adventure is about to begin.

ANOTHER COLLECTIVE NOUN FOR "QUAIL"

A bevy, a covey, a drift, a tremble of quail.

A MAIDEN AND HER SWAIN

A maiden and her swain carried the picnic basket between them across the meadow to the embankment, where they spread a cloth on the lush grass. The sun was shining, although this event occurred during the Dark Ages, which are called dark only because our information about that era is limited. It is we who are dark, then, not the age.

The meadow was an oasis, given that there were wars everywhere, just as there are now. Here and there were killing diseases and implacable famine. Superstition dominated people's lives. The end of the Roman Empire meant books had been lost, art was no longer classical, the elegant Latin language had lost its purity. It was as if intellectual curiosity and creative energy had died. It was as if all the people had gone to sleep, perhaps under a spell. Petrarch and Leonardo Bruni, those brilliant minds, were far in the future, as was the incomparable Dante. But some people longed for learning, a civilization that would lift them out of the mundane.

On the whole, the maiden and her swain were fortunate to live in England, where constant showers kept gardens moist, and patchy but reliable sunshine kept them growing. And no hardship can stop young lovers from loving. It might even push them closer in to each other's arms. How many soldiers have impregnated their girlfriends the night before they left for war?

No, the maiden and her swain have not yet consummated their passion. She is too smart to give herself away before he proposes. She has laughing eyes, long lashes, white teeth, skin as soft as a featherbed. He is nineteen, a fine figure, a trim six-pack, quick with words both wooing and witty.

Indeed, both of them love words. Puns, quips, double entendres, shaggy dog stories, they love them all. They love the sounds of words, the syllables, synonyms and antonyms. They like sentences, the more circuitous the better. But, as we have said, they are living in the Dark Ages and neither can read. Words on paper are merely squiggles. For that matter, there's very little paper.

The couple has eaten their modest lunch of bread, wine, grapes, and cheese. They lie in one another's arms. The maiden sees that her swain's cock is swelling. She sits up and points at it, smiling, but when he tries to pull her back down, she breaks away, laughing and teasing. She runs across the grass. He, of course, is obliged to wait until his member reduces. Then he gets up to race after her, and just as he does so, he sees that she has been brought up short by a white-bearded priest with alb and stole. He slows his pace and stands beside her.

The priest is telling the maiden that he can teach her to read. The swain leans in to hear better. He shares the maiden's dream.

The priest decides to give them a lesson then and there. "Amo," he says. "I love."

"Amo," the maiden says. "Amo," says the swain.

So it begins. Maiden and swain learn Latin at the priest's knee (they now sit under a linden tree in a three-cornered circle). As they learn the Latin names of things, each thing becomes brighter, like a candle kindling. After some months, the meadow catches fire, fish in the tumbling creek shine silver in the sun, and even the priest's beard is whiter than it was—as white as an angel.

And the maid and her swain? They still enjoy lying in each other's arms but now one reads to the other and the other reads to the one. They know so much now: Julius Caesar's wars, the tragedies of Sophocles and the comedies of Aeschylus, *The Consolation of Philosophy*. They are enlightened, and the Enlightenment has not even happened yet. The priest dies, and they weep for him, but they continue to read everything they can get their hands on.

One day the swain finds his scroll more difficult to read. Some of the letters are blurry. "I" and "L" are hard to tell apart. "Will you read this to me?" he asks the maiden.

She tries to, but the letters have become so small. "I can't read!" she wails, and though she is a cheerful, pleasant person, the wail is really a wail, a drawn-out, bitter, unmuffled, unmitigated suffering.

The swain holds her while she sobs. After a while he says, "We've lived too long. We've reached our Middle Ages. We've become short-sighted. Or maybe we have cataracts."

"Cataracts? What are cataracts?"

"Something that causes blindness," he says, knowing he is being redundant but thinking that the word will give her something to blame, something that's not him or her.

"Our lives are over," she says, noticing that the sky is getting darker.

"Maybe so," he says, still holding her, "but weren't they good ones?"

She smiles in spite of herself. "Very good."

"The best," he says.

"The best of the best."

And they finally made love.

LILING

During the early years of the Ming Dynasty, one young woman in particular was praised for her beauty. Of course there were other beauties, but wherever Liling went, admirers clapped, as if she were on stage rather than in her own life, or they bowed—and sometimes they did both—for they were captivated by her coiffed hair, her straight, small shoulders, her perfect, blushing skin, and her hands—so exquisite, so delicate, able to express everything in the most miniscule gesture. Liling leant on silken pillows embroidered with all the colors of the rainbow.

But she could not walk. At least not very far. Her feet had been bound at birth and now the deformed stubs at the ends of her legs could barely support her. Slaves bore her where she wanted to go, the poles of the litter supported on their shoulders, which in warm weather were oiled to glisten. In that case she would drape silk scarves over her face to prevent the sun from damaging her skin.

The purpose of binding women's feet, as I'm sure you know, was to make them attractive to men. The bound feet grew no longer than three inches. The permanent contortion of the foot excited the men, but why, I cannot say. Then again, with such small feet, the women's bodies swayed, sometimes precariously. The men liked that, found it erotic. It also allowed them to think that the women needed their strong arms. Parents bound their daughters' feet to ensure that they would find husbands with money.

Liling was happy, but, she thought, she would be so much happier if she could walk without always being about to tip over. She longed to explore the city on her own. She wanted to dance, if only for an hour. Her younger brother told her of his adventures in the city. How he ran and jumped and leapt over obstacles. How he climbed stairs and played games with his friends.

One day Little Brother came home wet. His hair was wet, there were drops of water on his *hanfu*. His feet were wet, his black cotton shoes soaked. "Where have you been, Little Brother?" Her voice was sweet, lulling, as it always was.

"Swimming," said Changming.

Liling knew that people who lived near the shore often swam, but her family were not near the shore. She knew that fishermen fished in the sea. She knew that fish and octopi swam in the sea. But—had Changming gone swimming in the sea?

"I'm learning," her brother said. "At school. At school I am learning to swim."

"At school? I thought you were studying letters and numbers at school."

"I am. But there is also swimming. We swim in the pool at school."

"The pool at school," she repeated, as if it were the most astonishing rhyme in the world. "The pool at school," she said again.

When her mother and father called Liling and Changming to dinner, she made up her mind.

"Papa," she said. "I want to learn to swim."

Her father's eyebrows went up. As if each were a little springbox or a rolled scroll.

"Females do not swim," he said, and his voice was low, as if he didn't want anyone to hear it. Maybe he thought a servant would overhear.

Liling adopted her calmest manner but she did not lower her voice from its natural range.

"I want to. I believe it will be good for me."

"Females have no need to swim," her father countered.

"I am female, Papa, and I have a need to swim."

Her father laid down his chopsticks and propped his chin on his hands. The rice in the centered bowl was still steaming. He brought his teacup to his mouth and sipped. At last he spoke. "What is this *need*?" he asked. "Have we not provided you with everything you need?"

"No, Papa," she said, not so much stubbornly as assuredly. "You see, my Lotus shoes"—by which she meant her deformed feet—"prevent me from learning about the world. And I am desirous of learning the world."

"Desirous," Papa said. "Perhaps you mistake the world for a husband. You will find a husband."

"Yes, Papa, I know. But first I must learn to swim."

Mama and Little Brother were as still as statues as this conversation continued. They were afraid Papa might stomp out of the room or lash out at Liling for her unconscionable request. Did she think she was above the rules? She was her father's favorite, yes, but he had to conform too. He too was bound—to convention.

"Must?" her father said.

"I am telling you the truth, Papa. You must take my word for it."

"*Must* and *must* again."

She said nothing.

"Your need is strong."

She looked straight into his eyes and did not flinch.

"So be it," he said, whereupon Mama, Little Brother, and even Liling relaxed their shoulders and sighed with relief.

The first time she dipped her foot in water she thought the water was like silk that moved of its own volition. It seemed as if a silk scarf were draped over her foot. She sat on the edge of the pool, that one foot—the right foot—dangling in water, and not until she became accustomed to the sensation did she lower her left foot. The water seemed to be cool and warm at the same time. Her brother demonstrated dog paddling, and then her father taught her to float.

She closed her eyes and she was floating on air. When she opened them again, she almost went under, but her father held her up with his strong arms and hands. Changming taught her the breast stroke. After she learned them, she practiced the breast stroke, the backstroke, the butterfly each day. It did not happen overnight, but eventually she had the hang of it. Now she felt as if she were crossing miles, though it was only the length of the pool. *Freedom,* she thought. *I now know what freedom is.*

Her small shoulders strengthened. She thought she might grow wings, because swimming was a kind of flying.

Did Liling drown? Her family may have thought so, but no, she did not drown. She swam the Yangzi. She swam the Nile. She swam the Mississippi and the St. Lawrence. She swam the Panama Canal and the English Channel. The Volga. The Dnieper. The Rhine. The Baltic Sea and the Vistula and the Seine. The Po and the Tiber. The Zambezi. She swam so far and so much that in time she forgot the names of some of the places she'd visited.

She skipped the Amazon. She had no wish to be nibbled to death by piranhas.

She never returned. She did not want a husband. She wanted to see the world.

Her parents missed her. Papa scolded himself for letting her learn to swim. Mama scolded Papa for letting Liling learn to swim. Little Brother would inherit all their earthly riches, which he would have gladly given up if only Liling came back. He missed his sister! Indeed, he missed her so much that he never again wanted to swim, not even in a pool. He thought it was his fault that she had gone away, and he'd been so proud of his big sister, her beauty, her intelligence. Her power, because he had felt that. Her power. Her strength. But he also thought: *She must never have loved us. Any of us.*

WHEN WE ARRIVED AT THE CASTLE

The heavy gates opened laboriously, as if burdened by worry. Men on horseback rode out to meet us, with iron masks, shields, and killing lances. The sun dazzled, reflected by chainmail. We made ourselves as still as death. A rider slapped us on the back and the world sea-changed from frozen to fluid.

THOMAS LEIGH

Suppose that slavery never existed in America. Suppose that all the Africans ripped from home and country and shipped to the Thirteen Colonies had been permitted to stay where they were. Suppose the slave trade had not exploded as a result of Southern planters needing cotton pickers. Suppose.

The man named Thomas Leigh, arriving in Virginia in 1785, would have found paid work on a farm, likely a tobacco farm. It would have been hard work, sweating under the boiling sun. It was a job that could make a full-grown man faint. A mean, hard, backbreaking job. But he would have known he was saving to have his own place someday.

The farmer he worked for would have chosen a day for a picnic, because he knew that if he wanted to keep his workers he had to provide some relief from the mean, hard, backbreaking work. And if all the workers knew one another, they would feel more at home and less apt to look for another job. He picked a day in late September, when it was still hot enough for lemonade and watermelon but cool enough that nobody had to suffer.

Thomas Leigh was glad for the break and happy to go to the party. He wore a clean shirt and carried a handkerchief in his pants pocket.

Thomas already knew the names of some of his coworkers, but not all of them. A curly-headed gal in a pretty pink dress snagged his attention. My, she was pretty! Her dark eyes danced. He about stopped in his tracks, just to look at her, but the boss farmer made the introduction. "Miss Tamasin Johnson, Mr. Thomas Leigh."

"How do you do?" Thomas said.

"I do just fine, thank you," said Tamasin. She seemed to be laughing at him but in a good way. Those eyes seemed to talk to him, the way they sparkled and twinkled like tiny stars. It occurred to Thomas that if she were to pin little bells in her hair, she would make music everywhere she went.

Of course they wound up talking with each other the whole time. When they went to their separate log houses, one for unmarried women, one for unmarried men, he asked if he could court her. "Now don't you think you should meet some other ladies afore you make that decision?" she said, but he could swear there was a wink in her voice, and he shook his head adamantly no.

"You may regret it," she said.

Whereupon he said, "Never."

They were married in a shady spot behind the boss farmer's house, under a maple tree that combusted into a fiery red in autumn. Tamasin wore a white cotton dress that her mother trimmed with lace and when she walked up to Thomas, beneath the maple and in front of the preacher, the groom once again thought he might faint. Was there ever, anywhere, a prettier girl? He thought not.

The first baby, a boy, came just nine months later. The second, a girl, put in an appearance before the calendar showed that another twelve months had passed. Thomas went to work whistling. Sometimes he sang. Gospel songs. To his children, lullabies.

Although Thomas Leigh was glad to have his job of planting, curing, and harvesting tobacco, he knew he'd better find something else if he wanted to stick around to raise his family. Just the smell of the stuff was enough to tell him that. His meager education had included reading. As soon as he could, he found work as a lawyer's researcher. Before he crossed the Atlantic, he'd dreamt of being an actor, but a family man had to take care of his family.

Ten years later he had six kids and a tidy sum of his own. With his money, which he carried on his person wherever he went, he bought a small house. It was plain to him that being an owner was more secure than being a worker. He carried Tamasin over the threshold. She wasn't as light as she used to be, but he thought it was good that she had gained some weight. A woman oughtn't be skinny. She should be able to jiggle some. A man wants to be able to rest his head on her titties.

Thomas was a happy man, bringing up his fine family with Tamasin at his side. He walked the children to school when they were old enough. When he came home, Tamasin had dinner ready. Winter and summer, his little house sheltered him and his from cold and heat and wild animals.

This is not to say that there were no troubles. The children were usually cheerful and polite but sometimes they got into rows that gave him headaches. One of the boys came home from a fight with a gash across his cheek. There were illnesses: chicken pox, measles. Once Vienna caught pneumonia; that was a horrid time, worrying whether she'd live. Thank God she did.

And then the children began to leave, one by one. They too found jobs, and sometimes the first job was farming, but Clayton worked as a cook and sweet Clover was a teacher in a private girls' school. Vienna married a boy both her parents approved of and moved all the way to Columbia, South Carolina; her young husband knew how to forge horseshoes and found work in a smithy, eventually garnering recognition for his magnificent metal workings of tools. Zandra married a homegrown boy who worked on a hog farm and every week brought home hog belly, fatback or, occasionally, pork chops. Jefferson, inspired by his father, studied law and became a full-fledged defense lawyer. Antonne was smart as blazes with wood and became a furniture maker; both black and white people clamored for his work.

But Thomas and Tamasin were now alone again, and this time they were a good deal older. Thomas's hair had turned white. Tamasin sometimes dyed her hair with henna, giving it a tinge of russet. Thomas was now a bit bent over—not so much as to seem painful, but it was certainly a herald of the future. Tamasin's hands and knees were stiff with arthritis. Yes, there were visits back and forth to see the children and grandchildren. There were birthday celebrations and holidays. And when there weren't, Thomas and Tamasin would sit in their rocking chairs on the front porch. But they were not fools. They knew that they were on the down side of the seesaw. It pleased them to know that their children were on the upside, but everyone knows that what the grim reaper does is grimly reap.

Tamasin took to reading the Bible. She had always been careful to read it to her children but now she turned to it for herself. Thomas would walk her to the church but he preferred to wait outside, even when it was winter. He wasn't a naysayer, but he felt more comfortable with nature than with God. Or maybe he thought God was more likely to turn up outside than in the church.

Tamasin went first. Breast cancer, but nobody said that word back then. The entire family surrounded her at her bedside, including Samuel and Vienna and their clutch of children up from Columbia. They buried her in the church graveyard. After the kids left, Thomas trudged home to his faithful house. The kids had brought all kinds of casseroles, soups, bread, and chicken dinners, but Thomas wouldn't touch any of it. He went outside, walked around the house, and came back in. He was sad, certainly, and disoriented without his wife. But he understood the order of things, the progression that life makes. He wasn't keen on dying, but he wasn't against it either. He was ready for it, and he looked forward to seeing his wife again, in Paradise. That is, if God didn't hold it against him that he had skipped all those church services, and he somehow didn't think God would. Why would a good God send anybody to Hell? Evil is its *own* Hell. Thus in time was Thomas reunited with Tamasin underground and overhead.

Suppose.

Clearly, none of this happened. Yes, there was a Thomas. There was a Tamasin. But both died early, poor, unmarried, childless, and enslaved, with bruises and weals and scars on their backs, arms, and hands. O America! We have sinned against our neighbor, whom we were meant to love.

LETTER TO JOHANNES GUTENBERG REGARDING PRINTED BOOKS

God bless Gutenberg, who began as a goldsmith and later, in Strasbourg, invented moveable type and thereby the printed book. We love books. We give them to people. We hoard them. We read them all the time, except, or even, when we are writing them. Books teach us empathy. Books inform us of many things. Books are lights that allow us to see the past, present, and possible futures. Books are knowledge. Books are adventure. Books are maps and surprises. Books are like crazy hats, eye-opening and catching our attention. Books make music. Some are solos. Some are symphonic. Some are like string quartets, taking us deep inside ourselves. Some are showpieces, like concertos. Duets and trios charm us. Short stories are sonatas. Some books sing, especially poetry books. Some books think, especially poetry books. Some books take a big breath and shout. Some books do mathematics or chemistry or paint landscapes. Some books look at books. A book enlarges the world, by whatever measure. But now we have eBooks, which we cannot smell or feel or turn the pages of, with footnotes that are difficult to get to, or, as we say latterly, access. Dear Johannes Gutenberg, please come back and bring with you the printed book.

KIERKEGAARD'S GAZELLE

The balletic gazelle traverses rough terrain in a leap that is like the Kierkegaardian leap to faith, whereby the mortal approaches, trembling in fear, a God who demands absolute commitment to what looks like a foolhardy, completely irrational risk, like the risk a gazelle takes as he seeks to outrun hyenas and lions, risk so great that it inspires anxiety and dread beyond bearing. This risk, the risk his God would have us take, is that of becoming a Knight of Faith. Who is the knight of faith? He who acts wholly, willingly, giving to God the totality of himself. Faith, Kierkegaard thought, would impassion us. Would move us from our modern alienation to engagement with God even in a faithless world. The horns of the Rhim gazelle curve backward like scimitars and yet he is as graceful as a lyric poem, or a ghazal. His coat is pale as sand. Kierkegaard loved to walk the twisty streets of Copenhagen. He was a fan of forgiveness and wished all would find it. Yet he believed that *infinite resignation* has to be reached before one can find faith. The Rhim gazelle matches the desert he tends to live in, the Sahara. He and his kind are endangered, mostly by hunters, and may by now be infinitely resigned. These gazelles are so beautiful that it hurts to look at them.

YOUNG MEN OF PRAGUE

Einstein and Kafka are young men. One, a former patent examiner and now a full professor, lectures on physics at the Karl-Ferdinand University in Prague; one, an insurance adjuster for the Austro-Hungarian government, sprawls in his chair at the café, a tall glass of lemonade on the table in front of him.

One lounges in his seat, dreaming of a young actress who travels with the Yiddish Theatre Troupe; the other runs a hand through his black hair and talks enthusiastically about atoms. The atom, he says, is a kind of dream, a space in which power is compressed to a point of conversion, at which point it becomes—becomes!—possibility. It is as if, he says, the atom is a symbol of itself.

The windows of the lecture hall have been opened wide, the shades snapped up. The pull-rings, wrapped in silk thread, can be reached only by a long stick with a hook on the end.

Beyond the windows, tall glasses of lemonade are growing downright hot atop the glass tables of all the sidewalk cafés. Trees in thick foliage shade the broad avenue and narrow side-streets, leaves rustling like taffeta skirts.

The sky is lovely, blue and silent.

To the young men, the sky is everything, a dream.

It is atomic.

It is theatrical—posed, awaiting a cue.

In the classroom, a young professor gestures, and tugs at his black hair almost as if he would absent-mindedly pull it out.

At one of the outdoor cafés, a young businessman drapes himself around his chair. The lemonade is stale and sour, and his digestion delicate.

So sweet, she is lovely, the actress, gentle and mirthful, her lips as red as blood. (Something wildly provocative about her mouth, as if she reddens her lips by biting them herself. . .)

The two young men, too, are lovely, in their fervor and good suits, and with such good manners.

Prague is lovely, a gold-leafed city dawdling on the far edge of the century now closing. There are so many books to be written, so many lives to be lived. So many dreams. The future is so close that for a brief moment there seems no need to hurry into it. In fact, there is a single moment when no one raises his eyes to look at it, just as a lover, sensing that the one he worships has at last arrived at the dance, chooses not to notice, attempting in this way to reclaim some of the control he has already surrendered.

Then, somehow, it happens that everyone looks up at the same time, which is what the darling beauty wanted in the first place. She shrugs off her wrap, into the waiting hands of the servant. She descends the short, carpeted staircase into the ballroom.

Everyone rushes toward her.

SIX WORDS

A murder of crows. Fallen feathers.

BROTHER AND SISTER

Syracuse, New York, 1940. She is five; he is twelve and newly aware of his dick, its ability to give him pleasure and confirm that he is male. He is so entranced by his genitals that he decides to show them to his sister. He walks nude into her bedroom, saying "Look at me." She looks at him. She is confused. "Why aren't you wearing clothes?" she asks. "Jesus, Margaret," he says, "I'm trying to show you something." "I see," she says, "but so what? What is that dangly stuff?" "It's what a guy has. Girls have a hole. A vagina." "A what?" she asks. "A *vagina*," he says. "Where is it?" Margaret asks. "Between your legs," he says. The dangly stuff stiffens. She watches it getting bigger. "Are you making it do that?" she asks her brother. "It does it on its own," he explains. "Don't you want to touch it?" "No," she says, shaking her head. "Why not?" "I don't know," she says; "it's strange-looking." "It's amazing. I think you should touch it." His dick is now quite large. "No," she says, not knowing exactly why she says it. Something about his entering her room. Something about his urgency, his excitement. He leaves the room, slamming the door behind him. She waits until he leaves the apartment. After he's gone, she shuts her eyes and pretends he never came into her room. He was not naked. She did not see anything, or not much. But when her parents return home, she finds herself telling them about it. They are appalled. When he returns, they chastise him. He cries, says he never meant to hurt her, will make it up to her. How? He will be nice to her, protect her on the playground, never ever do again what he did today. Never ever. Their parents are placated. He seems to have learned his lesson. Margaret, having told her parents, promptly forgets what happened. It is as if it never happened. He was never in her room. He would never do anything like that. Like what? She can't remember.

TODDLER

Two years earlier she'd been a rather rotund toddler in a blue onesie. Now she is a skinny four-and-a-half with long hair that seems to have a life of its own. Maverick, her mother calls her. Her father calls her Butch. It's true she's angry but she doesn't know why. Her parents ignore her but she's used to that; they have too much to do. At the same time, her parents scrutinize her face for clues to her feelings, and she hates that. It's intrusive! No, she doesn't know that word yet, but she knows what it means. She tries to eliminate all emotion from her face, to keep it still, composed, private.

A thousand years later she remembers a park. It may have been near a pond, or perhaps a curving road that made her think of a sea shore. A young lady with skin the color of chocolate milk crossed the park and came up to her. Was the young lady wearing an apron? There was something white in the scene but she doesn't know what. The young lady could have been twelve or sixteen or twenty-six, numbers that to the girl were just numbers. The lady held in her hands a tiny Easter chick dyed green. She opened her hands to let the four-year-old see. Did she give the chick to the girl? The girl doesn't remember, but she remembers worrying about the chick. Chicks were not meant to be green. Or perhaps she confused *dyed* with *died.*

But today, having lived a thousand years, what the girl mostly remembers is not the baby chick but the young lady. Who was she? Why did she bring the chick to her? Was she somebody's maid? Her family had no maid. Had she wanted to be friends? But how could the four-year-old be friends with anybody when she was always angry? She supposed the lady thought she'd want to see the chick, and it did fascinate her but she couldn't let anybody know that because the lady would take back the baby chick, or it would die. Anyway, something would go wrong. It always did.

THE NIGHT BEFORE CHRISTMAS

The Dunavant family lived in Philadelphia in an apartment building across the street from several businesses, and the sisters' room had a single window that looked out at the roofs. The sisters were five and eight. The eight-year-old had just turned eight and was quite proud of having reached such an advanced age. Her name was Charlotte; her younger sister was Catherine.

Their parents had chased them from the living room so they could put the presents under the tree. They always had a big tree, or so the sisters believed, but it may have been truer that the sisters were little. It was the night before Christmas and snow was settling, oh so quietly, on the roofs. And on the window sill, and the street and the sidewalks. It made the world look mysterious, which was how the sisters already thought it was.

Atop one roof was a neon sign. When had signs gone neon? It seemed a new thing, but perhaps the sisters had simply never noticed one before. This one flashed red on and off.

Not until they were in their last year of high school did anyone realize that the sisters were short-sighted. They were good students and always sat in the front row, so teachers just assumed that if they had sat in the back they would still be able to see the blackboard. But they would not have been able to do that, or to read the teacher's lips. And when they looked at the neon sign across the street, they could not see that clearly, either.

Each sister had her own single bed, both beds facing the window. Sitting cross-legged on her bed Cathy asked Charley if it was true that there was not a Santa Claus.

"Who told you that?" Charley asked.

"Some kids at school."

Charley, at eight, knew definitively that there was no Santa Claus, but it seemed sad to her that Cathy had to find out. "Oh, kids," she said, grandly. "They think they know so much."

"They don't?"

"They don't know anything. Look out the window."

Cathy looked out the window. The night was black. The snow was white and falling fast, blurring the buildings.

"You see the red? That's Santa's sleigh."

Cathy was dubious. "I don't know," she said.

Charley plumped her pillow. "Of course it is," she said. "He's stopped right next to the chimney, isn't he."

"Shouldn't there be reindeer?"

"The reindeer are covered in snow, that's why they are hard to see. After all, they've had a long trip and have to rest when they can."

"But—"

"Santa must be in the chimney. He'll climb back out soon."

Cathy squinted, the better to look for Santa.

Charley wondered how late it was. She had asked for a Donald Duck watch, and it would be so helpful to have it now!

The wind was picking up. It rattled the window in its frame.

"He should be coming up now," said Cathy.

"Maybe the people put out milk and cookies for him. He's probably hungry."

"The reindeers must be hungry too. Is anybody feeding them?"

"I'm sure Santa takes good care of his reindeer. He has to depend on them."

"And they have to depend on Santa. I still don't see him."

But just then a gust of wind made the neon sign blink. First it went dark, then it came back on.

"You see?" Charley said.

"See what?"

"Santa just got back into his sleigh!"

"I didn't see that."

"You'll see. There'll be toys under the tree when we wake up."

Cathy wanted to keep watching but her eyes had another idea: they wanted to close.

Both sisters were awake before dawn. This happened every Christmas Day. They were allowed to go into the living room and get their socks down from the mantel but not to make any noise or open any presents until their parents got up. They found an orange in the toe of each sock, jacks for Charley and a yo-yo for Cathy, small bags of M&Ms, new toothbrushes, a rag doll for Cathy and charm bracelet for Charley.

The snow had stopped. Presents weren't opened until after breakfast. The day went by quickly. Charley wore her Donald Duck watch and her charm bracelet on the same wrist. Cathy played with her rocking horse, hoping someday for a real one. She had seen a policeman on a horse and thought that's what she would like to be.

It wasn't until the holidays were over and they were in school again that Cathy said to Charley, "You lied to me."

Charley's face grew red.

"How could you do that?" Cathy looked as if she might be about to cry.

"I wanted you to enjoy Christmas."

"You shouldn't have lied."

"Wasn't it fun to think that Santa left the presents?"

"It wasn't true."

"But wasn't it *fun*?"

"It's not fun now."

Charley felt as if she'd done something awful or bad, maybe even evil. But had she?

Snow was falling again. From the living room she could see it swirling around the streetlight, the flakes like small white stars that had dropped from the sky. She didn't yet know that snowflakes are not white. That they are ice crystals. That her sister would never forget that she had lied to her.

ESKIMO BOYS

In the fifties, a boy of nine read a book about a boy of nine. The boy in the book was an Eskimo, probably Inuit, but Eskimo was not yet considered a derogatory term so the book called him an Eskimo. The boy in the book lived in an igloo. The boy reading the book lived in an apartment building with his father and mother. In the apartment, steam radiators kept their rooms warm, sometimes too warm. In an igloo, or snow house, the packed snow insulates the inside air, which can rise to 60 degrees. Sometimes a block of clear ice will serve as a window. One can lounge in one's nicely heated home and view the outdoors through an ice window.

The boy reading the book lived in San Francisco. Not in the city exactly but in one of its many suburbs. Sometimes his father or his mother—and sometimes both—took him into the city. He loved the streetcars and the steep hills, the fish market and the cool ways San Franciscans dressed, a tie with a tee-shirt, a girl in a man's suit, an old lady with three hats stacked on her head. They were "free spirits," his parents said, his father sighing, his mother pursing her lips.

In the book, words took up most of the pages, but throughout the book were sketches in light blue. A sketch never took up a whole page. A half-page rarely, a quarter-page more often. Perhaps there were ten or twelve sketches in all. The boy reading looked closely at each sketch. One showed how the blocks of snow were organized to make an igloo. He studied it carefully, wishing he could make an igloo. Another sketch showed the boy in the book wearing a fur coat sewn with bone needles. Outerwear was usually painted with pictures that told stories and were colorful, but the boy reading the book could only guess at the colors. Fur, usually squirrel or muskrat or sometimes mink, trimmed the hood, or "roof," of the parka. Grass was dried and then stuffed into socks for insulation. Fur-lined trousers were common. Still, one of the pictures showed the boy in the book wearing what looked like a long robe, and a cup was tucked into the crisscrossed top of the robe.

The book said that the boy in the book had been taught by his parents always to carry a cup when he went out. It was the custom, when one went visiting, to pull out one's own cup when offered a drink. Usually the drink was hot tea. The boy in the book drank the tea from his cup and caught up with the family he was visiting, especially the son, who was a friend and loved to fish. They swapped fish stories, and as they told them, the fish grew bigger and bigger until it resembled a whale, which, of course, is not a fish, and they laughed at themselves for telling such fantastic lies.

The boy reading the book in California wanted to carry a cup. He wanted to visit friends and tell fishy stories.

The boy in California looked through the kitchen cabinet that held cups and saucers, but they were either mugs—too big to carry in his jeans pocket—or delicate pieces of china that would make his mother truly mad if he tried to stick one in his pocket and broke it. Then he looked through the kitchen garbage can. There was just what he needed: a soup tin with the top removed. *Perfect*, he thought, and took it upstairs.

Of course, he didn't have anything like a long robe. He was wearing shorts and a tee-shirt and he tied the tin to his belt. All day he played in the backyard, imagining he was an Eskimo although the day was warm, and sticky with humidity.

It was still light when his parents came home. His dad had picked up pizza for dinner. His parents were silent all through the meal, and he didn't know why, but he seemed to catch the same silence-virus and found he didn't have much to say either. After dinner he went upstairs to read in his bedroom.

One of the light-blue sketches in his Eskimo book showed a sky with a cloud, the cloud shredded into thin bits by a strong wind. He imagined the North was always like this: cold, windy, ice blue. A cloud in tatters, a sky like a pane of ice a kid could look through. To what? He fell asleep, dreaming of what he might see through a window made of ice.

In the morning, he reached first for his tin-can cup. It was hanging from a bottom bed post. Something else was hanging there too: the cup, the actual cup, the real cup, the very cup that belonged to the boy in the book.

SATURDAY'S CHILD

On a morning in May, in 1953, my mother stands at the Formica counter in the kitchen of our house in Charleston, South Carolina, drinking cocoa and smoking a Chesterfield. She wears red lipstick, the only cosmetic she ever bothers with, the shiny tube a staple in her sleek white patent-leather handbag. If it were a weekday she would be getting ready to leave for work in the old Dodge, my father at the wheel, but it is Saturday, and Saturday means laundry, grocery shopping, changing the sheets on the beds. This early in the summer, this early in the morning, and it's already so hot a person could faint. She's wearing a straight linen skirt, dark brown with back kick-pleat, white blouse with a V-neck and batwing sleeves, and brown and white spectator heels, and despite the heat, despite its being Saturday, she wears stockings and a garter belt. She drags on her cigarette, douses it under the faucet. She drops the butt into the ashtray on the kitchen table on her way out. Though the screen door is latched, the back door to the kitchen is left open to let in a breeze, should there be, at some point, a breeze. In the side yard, a parasol of a maple tree spreads a circle of shade. The children use the maple tree as the starting point for games of Hide-and-Seek and May I? All day the children chase each other, laugh or cry, climb the monkey bars and swing in the swings. Or they go inside where they read books in their rooms while washing machines make a monotonous chugging sound downstairs. All day the children eat butter-and-sugar sandwiches made with sliced white bread that builds better bodies twelve ways. They drink bottle Cokes, the wasp-waist of the bottle fitting neatly in their hands though they do not stop to think about this. They race out again—letting the screen door slam and bounce, unlatched—and fling themselves down on the grass, blow milkweed puffs, braiding the ropy stems into bracelets. They practice screaming-in-terror so they can be in the movies. Screaming—the children have observed that this is what women do most in the movies. Actresses are supposed to be terrorized and scream, then fall backwards onto the bedspread. Playing cowboys and Indians, the children slip Indian-style, as they call it, through the yard, and the maple becomes their tepee. But after a few hours of make-believe they find themselves longing for their own lives, which, after all, are still new to them, unexplored and exciting. And so, though it is Saturday, they play school. They pretend it is a school day and that they are sitting at their small desks, working in workbooks. By mid-afternoon, the neighborhood is as silent as sleep except for the pencils being pushed across the workbooks. These kids know more than they would dream, as yet, of writing. They know that, everywhere they know of, there are expectations and practices with the force of rules. That there's not much difference between the pledge of allegiance and school prayer. People here hold revivals and save themselves. My mother thinks this is pretty idiotic. Pretty, but not completely. Since, she tells herself, the truth is you never know what the score is. But she doesn't tell anyone else that. As far as everyone else is concerned, she's got no use for wishful thinking. This is important to her: she wants everyone to know she has no use for wishful thinking. What she has is a boss who keeps trying to put the make on her. She has a new mortgage—this is the first house she and my father have owned—and she can't afford to lose her job. It's a long day. Saturdays are always long. She chainsmokes. By day's end, the bedrooms have been cleaned, the laundry and groceries put away, the trellis roses pruned and the dogwood trees trimmed, supper served and the dishes washed in the sink and dried by hand. She and my father sit for a while on the back stoop, cicadas and whippoorwills contributing background chatter as if they were guests at a cocktail party, but my parents don't throw parties. Live oaks scrawl shadows on the darkening sky. Magnolia blossoms rustle like silk, brushed by a stirring bird. My mother holds a Coke bottle in one hand, a cigarette in the other. She and my father talk. I don't know what they talk about; their voices are soft, and I am inside, on the other side of the screen door, deeply involved with a biography of Lou Gehrig. The stars come out one by one, like lights turned on in dark houses. Blue deepens into night, and at last there's a breeze. When I stand at my window, the air feels like chiffon on my face, billowing like cloth with the sighing breaths of honeysuckle, clover, scented by the dew gathering in droplets on the closed petals of the trellis roses, a perfume that should surely be called Evening in Charleston. My parents' voices are as soft as face powder, as if the South had rubbed all the r's and ending g's down to fine, dissolving outlines. My mother and father come inside and shut the back door. My mother hands the empty Coke bottle to my father and he rinses it out in the sink to keep the ants from being drawn to a sweet residue. There are speck-sized ants that find their way into the cabinets. We keep the lids on jars tightly screwed, the flaps on boxes closed, flour in the refrigerator. My mother crushes her cigarette in the ashtray. All those cigarette butts with red lipstick kissed onto them look like they're bleeding; like tampons. It's like a hemorrhage, that ashtray, like something bursting and flooding.

SIX WORDS

Squirrel leaps. Misses tree. Ghost squirrel.

VACATION

Skin-sations: how your skin feels when reassured by sunshine, brushed by a black-and-white feather, flicked by a fingernail. Sin-sations: delicious! Sun-sations: fun in the sun. Here we are, on the beach, in Unit #13. The sky is overcast. The surf roars out of the darkness with a white mane. Raindrops pelt the porch, roof, extended overhang. Our cottage is close to the edge of the ocean.

What is love, anyway? Does it matter if he would rather brood and drink than make love with me? If he busies himself all night with: hunting coquina; thinking about his father (bitter, depressed, dominating) and mother (with her expansive bosom and athleticism she would seem to have been made for high spirits, but no); thinking also about his daughters, who are now only visitors to his life, then back he goes to the cottage where he cooks up a batch of clam chowder, gleefully claiming it is the best in the world—"Not the best clam chowder but the best anything ever cooked," he emphasizes, mocking himself—and now he'll finish unpacking, pushing your things (too many, maybe too female) to one side of the shelf to let you know he has rights too, you are not the only person here for Christ's sake it's true you're paying for the vacation but who does all the cooking? Who takes care of all the details? Who takes the dogs to the kennel and who, let me ask you this, cooks the goddamn clam chowder?

And love? It's not sex; of which there is none. And God help us if it's romance, of which there's even less, though just last night there was a full moon that disclosed itself at the center of a circle of dark clouds and transmitted softly diffused moonbeams like delicate translucent elevators running between sea and sky.

He thinks I complain too much. I admit I find fault too easily, a trait I learned from my mother. Not only is it unpleasant for others to experience, it's a peculiar and pointless trait, since I am not often troubled enough by anybody or anything's faults to want to try to fix them. If something's not perfect, that's all right with me—as long as it is not some part of me that's not perfect; then I worry. And fret, and become angry and despairing, and piss people off until, before long, they turn away in disgust.

Otherwise, noting flaws is just reflex. It doesn't mean I'm unhappy.

I try to explain that to him. He refuses to believe it.

Is this love? We are more like roommates, defending our turf—sometimes from each other, sometimes, together, from the world.

If this is love, I would say that love's like time. It's always speeding up or slowing down, still ahead of you or already past. And it travels in only one direction.

Possibly sideways!

On the bias!

At a tangent!

I got up early and slipped out for a walk along the beach. Herring gulls and sanderlings hastened here and there over the sand. I found a black-and-white feather fallen among the shells and pebbles and picked it up and thumbed the fringe forward until it lay almost flat. Unit #13—from where I stood I could see the white plastic chairs on the deck, the jeans he wore the day before wrapped around a railing and meant to dry in the wind but drenched during the night, and the rain-soaked picnic table, of treated pine, dark and glossy as a Polaroid.

FOUR WORDS

People shoot. Guns survive.

SIX WORDS

Dead husband taught wife to shoot.

LIFE AT THE EQUATOR; OR, A METAPHYSICAL EXPOSITION OF THE CONCEPT OF LOVE

Time is therefore a purely subjective condition of our
(human) intuition (which is always sensible, that is, so far as
we are affected by objects), and in itself, apart from the
subject, is nothing.
　　　　　　　—Immanuel Kant, *Critique of Pure Reason*

I

Arriving at the equator, he set up a beach umbrella and a folding chair, and arranged himself in the folding chair in such a way that the umbrella shaded his face from the sun. The book that he placed open upon his lap and proceeded to begin to read was about love. He had a certain interest in love. He had never been in love, but he thought he might be someday, and he wanted to be prepared for the eventuality of that experience.

As the day wore on, it grew hotter. The sun beat down on the beach umbrella; the sand at his feet shone like glass. He was wearing sandals, white trousers, a white linen jacket, and a white shirt with a very pale yellow pinstripe. The shirt was open at his throat. He had not brought sunglasses.

Every day he arrived at his place at the equator, setting up his beach umbrella and his folding chair and taking out his book in this way. It was his habit. As dusk encroached and the many hidden birds and insects that live along the equator grew more vocal under cover of night, he folded his folding chair and the beach umbrella, and closed his book, and returned to his hotel, which was a mere fifty yards from the equator.

II

Life at the equator varies at different places along the equator; however, at any given point along the equator, the sun there rises at the same time every day.

One day shortly after the sun in this particular place on the equator had arisen, and shortly after the young man had arranged his chair, his umbrella, and his book and had begun to read about love, a young woman appeared. Her hair in all that bright light seemed startlingly dark, almost obscenely dark.

The young man at the equator watched the young woman settle herself at the equator.

The young woman, wearing a black bikini that set off her already accomplished tan, lay down upon a large yellow beach towel, caressed her bared skin with oiled palms, and, placing sunglasses over her eyes, fell, apparently, asleep.

Soon the young man realized that he was no longer reading his book about love. He was instead watching the young woman at the equator sun herself.

What country was this in? What year did these two meet? But these are irrelevant questions.

The next day very much the same sequence of steps took place. Once again, the young man discovered himself unable to concentrate closely upon his book, although he did make some minor progress. The young woman spent most of the morning lying on her stomach with the bra of her bikini unhooked, her back to the sun and to the young man.

On the third day, the young man approached the young woman, asked her if she would care to dine, and, happily learning that she would, folded his chair, his umbrella, closed his book, helped her with her beach towel and her bra and her sunglasses and her suntan oil, and escorted her to the dining room of the hotel some fifty yards from the equator.

III

The book about love which the young man was reading is titled *Life at the Equator.* In it, this passage may be found:

> People imagine that love is an emotion. They think that love is something they can feel, or that it is something someone may someday feel for them. Love is not an emotion. Love is a condition for the possibility of perception, as space and time, but preeminently time, are such conditions. That is to say, just as space and time are pure intuitions of the human mind, so love is a pure intuition of the human mind, a priori to any perception that the mind may seize or receive.
>
> Let us say even that the mind is located, is "geometrically" fixed, by a hypothetical outsider's constructing a triangle whose points are S for Space, T for Time, and L for Love. Should any of these points, S, T, or L, be absent, triangulation will of course fail, and the mind in question will remain outside the realm of the wholly perceivable, nor will it be able wholly to perceive the world beyond itself; in other words, it will be something less than really apparent and apprehending.
>
> Lacking the location in space, time, and love that would make it accessible to the perception of other minds, lacking the conditions by which fully to perceive the reality of other minds, it nevertheless may be real, to a degree if not to the highest possible degree, and consequently capable of affecting the world beyond itself.
>
> We may further designate the hypothetical outsider G (for God).

IV

At night, long breezes trail through the room, rustling, an anxious, silken sound that makes the young man dream of women in ball gowns waltzing on waxed floors above deep dungeons in large houses. Memory is a flower that blooms at night. A young woman and a young man will lie on sweat-dampened sheets, shower and dry themselves with a yellow towel while a monkey chirrs in a cage in the hotel's lobby and small, equatorial fish swim in an aquarium in their room. Clouds will rush by the opened shutters, threatening rain that will not come. In the morning, the sun will rise precisely at the hour and minute at which it arose this morning. The young woman will sun herself on the equator in her black bikini, her long black hair pinned above her nape, her eyes hidden behind black sunglasses. A young man dressed in a white linen suit and a white shirt with a pale yellow pinstripe will seat himself in a folding chair beneath a folding umbrella and begin to read about love.

THE TRAIN

I tell her we'd better hurry if she doesn't want to miss the train. It's late in the day.

I want her to take something with her, I want her to care enough about us to take something with her, some souvenir of her time with us, but the small suitcase I retrieved from the hall closet this morning and placed by her bedside is still empty. There is nothing, she says, that she wants to take with her. No handmade Mother's Day card she has hoarded since our childhood, no photograph or certificate of accomplishment. If she doesn't care about us, how about herself? But she doesn't want jewelry or makeup. How about a book, I ask, a souvenir of civilization? Civilization, she snorts. Her contempt is great. She says she is trying to get rid of things, not acquire them.

How stubborn she is, all seventy-eight pounds of her—approximately one pound for each year she has lived. She is intractable, a woman whose lack of sentimentality is more than defensive—it is aggressive, an act of force, hurls, has always hurled itself toward her family like a missile, an MX.

I am sentimental. I don't want her to go, I want her to stay, and I think that when she goes my heart will be ground zero, my chest will be an empty cavity like a shelled-out city, devastated, but I know that she has to go, even if she is frightened and would rather not, and although no matter when we leave we will be on time, I know that, by the same token, we must not be late.

I take my mother by the hand, help her rise and lean into the walker. Next, I help her into the car and place the walker in the boot.

As I walk around to my side of the car I glance up. Clouds push across the sky like boats across a lake. In their wake come bright breakers of light. This rippling light comes and goes as if the sun is a stone someone is skipping across the blue waters of the sky.

I slip into my seat, to the right of hers. She has gotten out of the glove compartment the small—no bigger than a walnut—brass ashtray that I bought her some years ago. It has a lid, which, though ill-fitting, serves to keep the ashes from falling out. She lifts the lid to flick her cigarette, lets it fall shut again. The ashtray won't hold more than two filtered butts at a time.

At this time of day, the road to Reading is clotted with commuter traffic. We pass the Cunning Man, the pub where my father used to drink a half-pint if my mother was in a mood and refused to fix dinner. In a mood, some nights she announced that hunger was a weakness, food disgusting. If people did not insist on eating, she explained, they would not murder the innocents of the earth, nor would they be so easily victimized by the unintelligent, who are in power everywhere.

My father, who died last year, was a sweet-tempered, largely unknown man who revealed streaks of sarcasm and bitterness only on the intermittent occasions when he'd had too much to drink. In his case, the third beer was too much—but my mother seldom let him drink it.

In the seat to my left, she is abstracted. I wonder if she, too, is remembering my father.

For my part, I find that it becomes harder to attend to the present as the past, on the march, swells its ranks, eventually dominating all time. The past has a territorial imperative, a mandate to annex the present. Memories overwhelm us; they grow so numerous that we have no time to think about anything else. They occupy us, like an invading army.

Yes, I am sentimental. I want to let nothing go. I don't want to let her go.

What are you thinking about? I ask.

And instead of saying, Hank, she says, Mama.

It has been troubling her that, no matter how hard she tries, she still cannot believe in God the way her mother believed in him. At seventy-five, she feels guilty that she used to say she was sick in order to stay home from Sunday School to read Grimm's fairy tales. Her mama always made her swallow castor oil, but she now feels that this was not a sufficient expiation. She wants to be six years old again so she can be the little girl her mother wanted, instead of herself. She would go to Sunday School; she would believe every word of the Shorter Catechism.

How, she asks me now, can she fail to share the beliefs of a woman who was perfect. Who was better than perfect, she says, who was good. I must be dense, she says about herself, this relentlessly un-dense woman, because after all this time, I still can't see it—and by "it" she designates whatever her mother found so persuasive.

She has tried, I know this. She recites the Lord's Prayer to herself every night, going over it word by word, trying to understand exactly what it meant to her Presbyterian mother. Thy will be done, on earth as it is in heaven, she says, wondering what that could possibly, really, mean. Is it gibberish, she wonders.

She is much more concerned with her feeling that she has somehow let her mother down, disappointed her, than she is with our feelings. I try to make allowances for this. I don't say it's ludicrous to feel guilt toward someone who's been dead for twenty-seven years. I certainly don't suggest that her perfect mother seems, imperfectly, to have saddled her with a sense of failure. My mother, who, within the limits of her circumstances, defied convention again and again, whose mind was extraordinary, berates herself not for not having been able, say, to revise her circumstances but for her inability to accept the world into which she was born.

Women do this, even unconventional women.

Her plight, its similarity to mine, to other women's, moves me. I am flooded with feeling—and know that she would have no use for it, would consider it a weakness. I want to touch her, but I am afraid to. Touching has never been permitted beyond hello, good-bye. There have never been congratulatory hugs, comforting pats on the head, reassuring arms around shoulders or even admonitory wrist taps. I try to do well what I'm allowed to do—I listen.

Her mother, she says, still on that subject, never missed a Sunday in her life. But because she was perfect, she wasn't forbidding, was never too-strict, never sour. She was fun-loving and sensual— though "sensual" is not and never could be my mother's word— and petite and auburn-haired; she loved to sing and dance, just as she loved to begin each day with a Bible reading around the kitchen stove. Obadiah and oatmeal, early every morning.

The clouds have lifted, and now, as often happens in England, there is a late-day reprieve from existential gloom, a sky like British empiricism, clear and comprehensible, uncontinental. For a few moments, as we inch our way out of the car into the station, it is almost hot, or at least we are almost too warm, in our long sleeves and wool coats, beads of perspiration creeping out from under our arms like secrets desirous of being told. Then dusk, slowly at first and then more quickly, begins to steal the warmth from the air.

The station itself is cold, like a meat locker. I feel the cold concrete under my shoes' soles; the walls sweat like meat, damp leather and fur coats give off a dead-animal smell. On the first platform inside the gate, people bench-sit, warming their fingers around Styrofoam cups of steaming milk-thick tea.

She stands in her walker, a sailor in her ship's crow's nest ready to shout ahoy, while I step over to the sweets counter and load up on Cadbury's. It's the one thing I can be sure she'll eat— she likes her chocolate.

Now starts the long struggle down stairs and through the underground passage to emerge on the other side of the tracks. This part of our journey consumes a great deal of time and energy. By the time we are on the relevant platform, the 5:06 to Paddington—the train my parents used to take to London when they were going up for a concert—has left the station. More trains enter and leave. At this hour, the service between Reading and London is intense.

None of these trains is the one we are waiting for. My mother sits on a bench, nibbling chocolate. She breaks a tiny, dainty piece off from the bar and scrapes a few slivers from it with her teeth and swallows them, her hand in front of her mouth as she swallows because she does not like for anyone to see her eating, ever.

In the past few weeks, I have had to bathe her, help her to the commode chair, hoist her on and off the seat. I know exactly how thin she is: as insubstantial as if she were her own silhouette. I know that her buttocks are as small and pointed as elbows. I know that her skin, turned to parchment by cortisone, will barely stretch across her body without tearing. She will eat a six-minute soft-boiled egg if it is served just so; otherwise, she subsists on cocoa and candy bars. Her hazel-green eyes have ghosted into gray, clouded by failing vision. She is almost deaf. All her senses are withdrawing from the world, pulling away—as if her body is finally concurring in the conclusion her mind drew long ago, that the world is not worthy of her attention.

I want to say something to her, I want her to talk to me, but she just sits there eating Cadbury's, while the station empties. Pretty soon we are almost the only ones left on the platform, and it's dark now, electric lights shining in the newsstand, the miniature cafeteria.

Don't you miss Daddy? I ask her. The question flies out of me as if it has wings, as if my mouth is a sprung cage. I stand there astonished, gaping, imagining my question on the loose, on the lam like an escaped canary. My tongue feels thick, too big in my mouth, it feels like feathers, I can't get another word out, I'm thinking she has a right to be angry with me, offended. I am presumptuous.

But I don't dare ask her what I really want to ask her. Asking her if she misses him, what I want is for her to answer what I'm really asking her. What I am really asking her is if she will please say something to me that proves that all this caring, all this loving and losing and missing of one another that we all do, means something, that it's not just incidental feelings that happen to go along with events that happen to happen. I think she ought to know. I think she's lived long enough to know.

I want to hear my mother say that my father was not just a random factor, that he was an essential part of the equation of her life. She is licking her fingers. She is in no mood for metaphor. Metaphor is not what is real to her at this point.

Mama, she says, sighing, Mama was so pleased with me for marrying him, even if she did act matter-of-fact about it. Mama never let anything ruffle her. She took me downtown and bought me a trousseau for twenty-five dollars. And Papa was ecstatic— his little Eleanor was marrying a violinist! His daughter, the sawyer's daughter, and her handsome husband would play their violins, and they would never have to resort to mere language for conversation—that was pretty much my Papa's idea of heaven, so he thought it was a marriage made in heaven. But Mama approved of my choice because he was a Presbyterian. There! You see, she says sharply, wiping her hand on the front of her coat, even your father was able to believe. I am sure that he did, even though he would never talk about something so personal. He was just like Papa in that—wouldn't talk about anything like that. She is folding the foil and colored wrapper around the remainder of the candy bar, tucking it in her pocket, without looking at what she is doing. What if they are all together and don't want me with them? she goes on, and now her hands are folded, fingers interlocked, as if in prayer, but almost immediately she pulls her hands apart again and, with crossed arms, slips them up the inside of her coat sleeves in the smallest of self-hugs. What if I'm not permitted to join Mama? She starts to cry but stops. It would be just like the God of this world, wouldn't it, she says, sarcasm pulling her face into a hard mask, setting her features like cement, to make heaven, if there is a heaven, a club for believers.

Her eyes fill up again, puddles in her face. I hope Mama will forgive me, she says, for not living up to her expectations.

I look at those gray eyes and say, I'm sure she forgave you a long time ago.

Her face settles back into itself and an intent waiting.

It's as if my father has lost his connection to her as husband, even in memory, and is important only as someone who once had an effect on her relationship to her parents. He was one of their sons-in-law, that's all.

Now the train is coming, it is a zipper pulling into the station on the seams of the tracks. She hauls herself up into her walker and starts to stumble toward the train. Wait, I tell her; there's plenty of time, they won't leave without you, but she is afraid that she won't make it to a smoking car, she has to get on a smoking car.

We find a smoking car and the conductor helps us get her on. I want to get on too, settle her in her seat, but he says, No time, no time.

And he is telling the truth, for when I look around, I discover, much to my amazement, that the station, which had been deserted, has filled up again, passengers are clambering aboard, so many many passengers/where have they come from, and then what is happening becomes clear to me in a way that I had refused to let it be clear before, as I look down the length of the train, toward the engine, and I see face after face that is dear to me, all the lost people of my time, the missing souls.

And now I am frantic, my heart feels as if it is going to explode, it is a time bomb that has been rigged in my chest.

She is by a window, staring forward. I run to the window and stand on tiptoe and knock on the pane. She turns to me and smiles distantly and turns back, staring ahead. The sleek body of the train is cold fire under my palms as I lean into it, as cold as her flesh. She's not even looking at me. I pull away from the train and throw myself into a pantomime, waving don't go, and then I am shouting don't go, and it's all happening too fast—how can things be happening so fast? While we were waiting, everything seemed to be in slow motion, but now it has all speeded up and though I am shouting, though I am crying and calling to her, no one is paying any attention to me, they are all busy busy busy, the conductors must keep things orderly orderly orderly say the wheels.

No time, luv, no time.

The engine is starting, the train is like a long, lighted tube sliding through the station, and I reach for the door but it's too late, the train is leaving and my mother is on that train, she is going away, she is not even interested in staying. Children, what are children? Afterthoughts, byproducts. . . . Late, they arrive too late on the scene to be of consequence. She had prior commitments and she is going to meet them.

How dark it is, the train streaming out of the station into the night like a river rushing into the ocean! All at once, there is nothing—only the thin whistle of wind as it falls back from the outbound train, the dull echo of my heels on the concrete platform.

She is gone.

It's over.

I am completely alone on the platform. Not one other person remains.

I look around and I feel vulnerable. This is not a safe place to be, I realize. Not safe. I start down the stairs, to cross over to the exit.

It's so dark in the tunnel, I scurry through it like a mouse. I want to be with people, I want to talk to someone before her gone-ness becomes more real than her going-away. I want to review her going-away again and again so I won't have to feel her gone-ness. I want to talk to someone who will listen to me as I try to convince myself that it's not possible that someone who existed can not exist. I will say I believe it's not possible that we have been sent on a journey to nowhere, and the way there is marked more by farewells than welcomings.

Such a long, sad journey—and she is taking it by herself, on that train, seat next to the window. As I leave the station, my used bystander's ticket crumpled in my pocket, I think how brave she is, how brave we all are, people, all of us people alone and dying, now and forever alone, brave beyond belief.

I don't say any of this to anyone. There is no one to say it to, and if there were, I still wouldn't say it. It is much too personal.

I get in the car, in the parking lot, and turn the ignition on. The small brass ashtray, one cigarette butt, is sitting on the ledge in front of her seat on my left. I put it away in the glove compartment. She took nothing with her.

A DREAM WITH THE WIND IN IT

After their deaths, her parents still visited her. Well, mostly it was her mother who came. Even when her father tagged along, he tended to stay off by himself, in a corner. As he'd always done. Her mother would come up to the foot of the bed and call her name until she woke up. Though the room was dark, her dream was suffused with reflected light, a dreamy moonlight, and Michelle could see her mother, who was wearing a workshirt and underpants, clearly. She used to walk around the house like that when Michelle was a teenager. The shirt was one of Michelle's father's shirts, with the sleeves pushed up.

Each time, Michelle asked her mother what she wanted, but her mother never answered. And yet her mother seemed so sad that Michelle was sure that she must want something, and it drove her a little crazy not to be able to figure out what it was, because it must be something she expected Michelle to give her. An apology, perhaps. Or forgiveness.

Or love.

But Michelle had given her so much love when she was alive.

But perhaps it had not been enough.

Perhaps it was never enough.

In the morning, lying in bed, Michelle watched the green sleeves of the linden brushing her window. Even with all the traffic noise—the angry rush and howl, the scowl, of it—she could hear the birds' grace notes, trills and frills. And still, in this light, her parents were there, though fainter, like blood spots fading with time.

Pale as a memory from childhood, her mother was leaning toward her, and calling her name, and Michelle heard it like a wind from a place that was always cold, even in early summer.

She lived in Pierre, South Dakota. She worked for a cartage company, invoicing householders arriving in town, departing town.

One night Michelle woke to her name being called, and in the moonlit dark she saw her mother painting the walls of the room white. Paint stuck in her mother's hair like bird droppings and frosted her mother's bare legs, her no-nonsense forearms. The hairs on her mother's arms were like the gleaming branches of a tree after an ice storm. She asked her mother why she was painting in the middle of the night like this. Her mother turned around and seemed about to answer, but all she said was Michelle's name, again, and while it was all right to hear it like that in the dream—which was not quite a dream—it made a sound like a draft of wind, and it chilled Michelle, it really did, even in early summer.

It was the way her mother said it, as if she were deeply lonely in death.

And yet Michelle's father, too, was there. Her father and her mother were together, as they always had been.

Michelle woke, feeling a prairie wind sweep across the deserted terrain of her heart. She thought of her mother and father and how alone each must have been in life. She saw the linden leaves casting a latticework shadow on the white walls of the bedroom, and she heard the birds in concert. She wanted to tell someone she was innocent. It wasn't my fault, she wanted to say, but to whom could she say it, ever? And when she tried to say it, aloud, there in the room by herself, it came out sounding like her own name, like the name Michelle.

One night as she lay in bed, Michelle saw her mother's breasts—wilted, in old age, like flowers past their bloom—try to fall forward, but they were like two flaps of skin with no fat inside. Her mother straightened up again and the breasts somehow folded themselves back upon her mother's sternum, flat as a child's, and her mother's arms became wings folded into her sides, and now her mother was a vulture, huge and impassive, waiting at the foot of the bed.

Then Michelle heard a voice and thought it was her father's, thought the place he was calling from was cold and dark, with a wind reaching out of it like a tempest. Her mother touched Michelle's foot with an outstretched wing, and Michelle felt that the voice and the touch were going to take her away, the wind was going to bear her away. She knew she had to lift her eyelids, even though the force of the gale pushed them shut. Making an enormous effort she opened her eyes, and it became clear to her that the voice she heard was her own, calling to her out of someplace cold and dark inside herself.

Michelle woke, and it was night—or it was morning—and—whether it was night or morning—she was always cold, even when the birds sang, the cardinals like blood spattered on the sky. Once, her mother was running up long columns on the adding machine; once, she was stringing bones on the clothesline in the back yard.

In the moonlight the bones were as white as if they'd been painted. Michelle watched her mother in the yard, the long, shapely legs bare and foreshortened beneath the workshirt.

It was as if her mother were dancing down there in the yard. It was as if her mother were busy with some important work of art.

She wondered how her mother could be so energetic, so enthusiastic about whatever it was she was doing. It took all the energy Michelle had, it seemed to her, merely to sleep each night and dream, a dream with wind in it, a dream that could carry her away.

SPEAKING VANISH

. . . they discussed the strange light on the sea . . .
— Anton Chekhov, "The Lady with a Dog"

Cyrena, curator of a small community-college museum in Houston, had gone as a member of a cultural exchange to the then-Soviet Union to view the work of emerging Russian artists. Her group had stopped in Moscow before heading south to Yalta. In Moscow they'd read an announcement in the paper: "There will be a Moscow Exhibition of Art Workings by 150,000 Soviet Republic painters and sculptors. These were executed over the past two years."

An Armenian sent flowers to her at the station in Moscow, which she received as she was boarding the train. In Yalta a Tatar serenaded her from beneath her balcony.

"Did I tell you about the day we danced on a Spanish galleon moored in the Black Sea during a rainstorm?" Cyrena asked her friends at lunch at Botticelli's. They had an hour for lunch.

"A Spanish galleon?" asked Wade. He was the librarian for the museum.

Narciso, a professor of Romance languages, said, "One of my students once translated a line into: They all cry out in French and vanish. Are you sure it wasn't a Vanish galleon?"

"It was a movie set," Cyrena said.

"Tell us," Wade begged.

Then Cyrena told them how she and three other Americans, archaeologists, art historians, or gallery owners, guests of the Soviet

Museum Curators and Finders-Keepers Union, had gone out on the Black Sea in a small motor launch with their hosts and gotten caught in an impromptu squall. The First Mate—who was also responsible for security in that area—which was an area where Party bigwigs, including, in the old days, such luminaries as Khrushchev, had their dachas—anchored the boat beside the galleon, which they all scrambled onto. On the galleon there was a room with a roof, an office actually, because this was, after all, a movie set, not a true galleon, despite the topsail and rigging, and the waves roiling around the hull. Someone turned on a radio, someone else produced a bottle of vodka, which he had thoughtfully liberated from the guest house, and the dancing began. Cyrena was wearing forties-style shorts that flared out from her thighs like a skirt and came almost to her knees, but everyone else was in a bathing suit. The First Mate, with grizzled hair on his chest like the fur of a bear, and rounded bearish shoulders, and pawlike hands, and flanks like bear steaks, wore an itsy-bitsy teeny-weeny yellow polka-dot bikini. He did! He enfolded Cyrena in a bear hug and spun her like sugar, as if she were as light and airy as cotton candy, around the phony wine kegs and real portholes. He was not troubled by being shorter than she: At five-three-and-a-half, she was, at last, a tall American success story. Someone handed her a glass of vodka with a green pepper in it, the green startlingly vivid in the silver glare of the cloudy sky. There was bread with salt on it to follow the vodka. The rain on the roof sounded like machine-gun fire, as if the civil war everyone thought might happen had already begun. Everyone on the esplanade these days was talking about the coming winter, food shortages—maybe famine—the threat of a military coup, and the Mafia, who seemed to be everywhere.

The rain was pockmarking the Black Sea, and the happy First Mate was doing the twist in an itsy-bitsy teeny-weeny yellow polka-dot bikini, and Cyrena had managed to pull away from him and was standing at one of the portholes, looking out over the choppy water at the Crimean Mountains that encircle Yalta, finding them mysterious and haunting, as ancient as awe, Gilgameshish, the sun reappearing now at the end of the day, a light opening up like a tunnel in the sky leading back, back, back into time, back to the beginning of time, where everything that was, is, and everything that will be, has been. It seemed to her that it was a sacred place, a place where the holy breaks through, a place where eternity breaks through. The sky was full of seagulls, a summit of seagulls. Dolphins danced in the sea off the starboard side.

One of the Americans, whose specialty was the deciphering of classical inscriptions, talked about meeting Robert Graves, who was by then already an old man. "He kissed my hand and said he wished he had met me earlier," the epigrapher said, still amazed after all these years. He shook his head, bemusedly, a scholar who had once been taught a lesson about the love of knowledge, how it embraces the whole world, asking nothing in return.

The cloudburst slowed. They all held towels over their heads and dashed back to the motorboat. In the cabin, garbage pails overflowed with apple cores, scraps of bread, half-drunk paper cups of pineapple juice spiked with vodka, in which Crimean insects had drowned, going down to a sticky death. The day itself felt left over, a scrap of time that no one quite knew what to do with, how to make use of, and yet the suffusion of light was like a sign—if they could only interpret it—an iconography of light, widening and widening. Cyrena remembered the light changing then, spreading across the sky like wings, and how it flew off down the long tunnel of itself, into night.

And the water was cold and deep, the Black Sea black.

NOSTALGIA OF THE INFINITE

Two people break up. The one who didn't want to goes on loving the one who wanted to, but her love for him is a bone she buries next to her heart. It's still there.

REUNION

She brings him African violets, geraniums. A breeze from the harbor nudges the white curtains aside, probes. Sounds—a crying gull, a screeching car alarm, the pneumatic gasp of bus doors opening and closing—are separate and distant, like islands: they do not touch this couple brought together after so many years, do not impinge. Within the room, the only sound is of the lifted curtains snagged and pulling briefly on the geranium and then sliding free again. And his breathing, of course. She listens, and the room seems to her as glaring as a tropical beach: white sheets, white walls, white bureau, the white curtains rising and falling as if breathing too. Beyond the room, she knows, everything is blue: blue sky, blue water. Waves rubbing against the hulls of boats like cats winding around people's legs. But not tropical: this reunion takes place in New Jersey, a place that to her seems like an outpost, the last and farthest place she could imagine herself in.

She smooths and tightens the sheet, fits it more closely to his sides. The chemo caused his hair to fall out months ago. His large head is now the most aggressive thing about him, physically large and intellectually dominating. Though he was always intellectually dominating! She would like to be able to read his mind. She would like to be able to turn the pages of his mind. Know how the story began. How he summarized it to himself.

How it ends.

The dark eyebrows, the gaze which, in those early years of discovery and argumentation, of shaping a self, had hurled itself against its object. . . .

But now his eyes are shut, the lids thin as thread darned over holes in a sock heel.

Until early evening, she sits beside him and reads to herself. The white light turns bluer, as if a mistake has been made *something has gotten mixed in that should have been kept separate a blue bleed in the laundry the whites gone aquamarine and watercolor.*

Quite suddenly (but it has gotten late), it is dark.

A waltzing blackness. Then an orderly switches the hallway lights on.

She slips her book back into her bag. She has rented a room in the kind of motel where people stay for a week, spending their days at the shore and never going out at night but instead heating up tasteless microwave macaroni-and-cheese to dine on in front of the television; how else can a single woman (all these years when they would have been married, if he hadn't panicked and run, a young man afraid he had lost himself, his future, well, what future now!) afford a vacation? Not that this is a vacation, and not that the only people registered here are beach-goers. There must be others, like her, visiting the sick, the discouraged, the sad, the doubtful. She leans over the figure in the bed. She kisses him on the lips and it is like kissing a thought, not a person. She traces the curve of his large head from the temporal lobe to behind his ear, and it is like touching the idea of a man but not the man.

She makes a small sound in spite of herself, a short cry as if she is a sort of gull; as if she is a kind of island despite literature, and each slowly falling tear is like a drop of water on a laboratory slide. She imagines herself viewing her tears under a microscope. In her tears she would be able to see the biology of him, the way he used to be, hot-tempered and verging on violence, his dark, mole-bedecked skin, the contained, tumultuous blood, the nerve-endings that were as brilliant as stars.

The many constellations of them, their synapses, designs and meanings, and do not forget the neurotransmitters as swift and showy and portentous as comets.

But she remembers that when they were together she let it slip that she didn't think he was as intelligent as others thought he was and certainly not as intelligent as he thought he was. *You must never belittle the male ego*, her mother once told her, but she, of course, she, herself, thought her mother was foolish, unliberated and not up to date. Well, her mother had been right. She had to give her that. Her mother had known whereof she spoke, didn't she.

If she could have him back, she would admire everything he accomplished, praise him unstintingly. By now she knew no one was hugely intelligent, much less herself. Definitely not herself. What a waste of energy it was to worry about intelligence. A waste of time, too.

She moves back toward the hospital bed. If he opens his eyes, she will tell him he was the most alert man she ever knew. She will tell him she never stopped loving him. She will tell him how painful it is to live with her guilt. She will

HOW SHE'S CHANGED

He begged for her love. She gave him her heart. He spat on it, stomped on it, kicked it and threw it out the window. Now she's heartless.

FOUR WORDS

Looking for love, blindfolded.

FIVE WORDS

Woman, sawed in half, exeunt.

AQUARIUM

In the aquarium there was a green moray eel as wide as a man's necktie from the nineteen-seventies.

There were fish—not tiny, not big, merely mid-sized— swimming from just below the surface to just above the bottom and there was a faux bridge to swim over and under and across and other things meant to make fish feel at home, though who knew what made a fish feel at home, except a fish. Maybe not even a fish.

The couple stood close to the saltwater aquarium, holding hands.

The woman was looking at fish swimming on the right side of the aquarium, but her husband was watching the fish in the upper left quadrant.

"Oh my god," her husband said.

"What?"

"They are ganging up on him." And sure enough, when she looked at the spot he was pointing to she saw four or five fish nipping at a smaller, but still mid-sized, fish. Each time the smaller fish tried to stay with the bigger fish, they butted him and nipped him and he floated downward, as if drowning, but fought to rise again, and they butted and nipped some more and then he drifted to the bottom of the aquarium and was still.

"Dammit," her husband said.

"Tell someone," she said.

Her husband pointed out the aquarium situation to the waiter, who was Hispanic and had a sweet face. The waiter went somewhere else to tell someone else.

The woman was unsure when she and her husband had stopped holding hands. It had seemed disrespectful, or too self-involved, to hold hands while the bigger fish were ganging up on the smaller, but still mid-sized, fish. "I never knew that fish would do something like that," she said.

"You didn't?" he asked. "It's a fish-eat-fish world, you know."

"I know, but—" But what? she wondered. "That they would gang up like that?" she said, tentatively.

"Everybody's a bully," he said. "When they have a chance."

"You're not."

He took her hand again and kissed it. "That's some eel," he said.

"It looks like a man's tie from the nineteen-seventies."

He looked back at the aquarium. "Damn if you aren't right," he said.

But she was too sad to say anything else.

SIGN ON NEW YORK CITY BUSES
IN THE SEVENTIES

Please let those who are getting off first.

LANDING MILES

Goldie's Bangs's first love was books. One of the fringe benefits of marriage to Miles was that she got to stay on at the college after she was no longer a student. Every day she went to the campus coffee shop for lunch. Rainy days were mostly spent in the reading room of the library. Other days, she would go for walks in the woods that camouflaged the tennis courts. The campus was shaggy, ragged. Roses climbed the porchwalk between senior dorms, and halfway down the hill there was a remodeled carriage house for the luckiest students. She had been one, and a senior honors student. She'd shared a room on the top floor with Betty Lou Baranov. In those days they played *The Four Seasons* day in and day out, and she still heard the massed strings in certain weather, or, hearing them on the radio, instantly remembered how the dewy roses smelled in the early hours of a long day unbroken by classes. And in the redolent air of late summer and early autumn her stride lengthened and she felt energetic and anticipative, as if nothing was impossible. She still felt that way more often than she could tell Miles. He knew her instinct for freedom and was afraid she would act on it—he had told her so. What she couldn't get across to him was that the freedom she sought wasn't social; it had to do with the sense she had, at certain entirely unexpected moments, that she was on the verge of breaking out of her own body, so that if she could only find within herself that minute but absolutely crucial missing force and bring it to bear, she might escape herself once and for all and experience life directly, free of the distortion that went hand in glove with sensory mediation. She considered her body a clumsy thing, a nuisance at best and on occasion the worst dampener of her spirit there was, since it impaled her upon fallibility as finally as the butterflies in her collection were pinned in their cases. If Miles said she was as pretty as the North Star on a clear, frosty night, she was grateful for the truth of his statement but knew it to be beside the point. His love for her made her impatient.

It was five o'clock, the hour when shadows take on new shapes, become deeper, wider, more profound. The birdbath in the backyard had been vacated. Silence hung from the sky like sheets from a clothesline on a still day. Goldie gnawed the skin at the side of her thumbnail. Miles was in Newport News, attending a symposium on marine biology, and wouldn't be back until morning. She fed the hamster and the budgie, went outside to switch on the sprinkler system, and returned to the article she was reading. It was on the phenomenon of phosphorescence, and put her in mind of the first term paper she'd ever done for Miles. She had been trying to get his attention, but without success. Even though it was supposed to be a major *faux pas* to call a man, she had considered doing it, but she thought she might scare him off. But she could do something outlandish with the term paper and he would have to sit up and take notice. Using the red half of her ribbon, she'd typed the title on a page by itself: "Are Fish Human?" Ten pages later she reached a conclusion. "On the best available evidence, then, it seems safe to say that, all things considered—all relevant things, anyhow—fish are not human, and are not likely to become human in the near future, though they may have done so in the past." He refused to give her a grade on something so off-the-wall but asked her out. He was handsome, shy, a master of flourish, the confirmed bachelor surprised by circumstance. She was the circumstance. Betty Lou said rumor had it that Dr. Bangs carried a torch for a Norwegian. That had made Goldie suspicious of her own good looks: Her hair was so bright it blurred into silver, like the sun at noon. Except on the hottest days she dressed in blue jeans and a red plaid Pendleton shirt. The sleeves were too long and had to be rolled up; but then, in other weather, she could pull the cuffs down over her chilled fingers. She spent a lot of time outdoors— the outdoor world was a gift from her father, a rancher in Arizona, and one of the things she and Miles had been quick to share with each other. She loved the outdoors almost as much as she loved books. It was as if Miles had given her the same perfect present a second time, with all the delight from the first intact, but this time the present came wrapped in Linnaean nomenclature, similarity and difference categorized and clearer than ever. "Look at this," Miles said; "see here and here." And everywhere she looked, the clouds opened or the trees bent back or the waves parted to let her pass. She decided she was chosen. Surely anyone would have, in her shoes. Chosen for *what* was an altogether different problem. Insofar as purpose was allied to function, it was in fact the problem of classification.

There were short-sighted skeptics who thought that classification was a supererogatory exercise, unnecessary and misleading. A rose by any other name would smell as sweet, wouldn't it? But perfume was not the point but only a secondary characteristic. Goldie knew that the point was in the naming, and that Adam and Eve, assigning birds and beasts to their proper phyla, had themselves co-created the universe, however fractional a part of it Fredericksburg might be. They were the first and quintessential scientists. Shamed by knowledge, they were raised up by the utter bravery with which they confronted more of the same, moving on into that tangle of theory and fact that stretched out from Eden like scrub country. Nobody knew what lay out there: flash floods, drought, and sudden drops off the scale of probability into the absurd. The rose was a rose until one day it wasn't, becoming instead a new and subtle variant with a treacherous tendency to cross the boundaries of established category. Viruses are living organisms, when they aren't inanimate objects, complex proteins. Light is a particle, when it isn't a wave. Like induction itself, science could be trusted only so far. Beyond that point, the gates closed on Paradise, and you were on your own in unsettled territory, and the sun might rise tomorrow, and then again it might not. Some days you couldn't even know for sure whether the sun shone or didn't. On a warm and windy day, when the light was as skittish as a colt, Goldie had gone to the class picnic with her handsome fiancé. So many changing shadows, ducking here and there, put her in a playful mood, and the quickening breeze lifted the hairs on her arms. She felt as buoyant as the milkweed blown on the current by the faculty kids. Her engagement ring winked and seemed alive, like a drop of pond water under a microscope, as she came up over the hill and joined Miles under the mulberry tree. He was talking to Christian Turner. "—Sonja," she heard Christian say. Goldie didn't like the man. His voice was too loud, and he had a habit of sucking his lower lip between his teeth, as if to suggest something. "What about Sonja?" she asked, coming up next to Miles's shoulder. "Sonja who?" "Oh," Miles said. When he waved his arm, as if to brush the question off, he hit her in the stomach. She laughed. There was a pause. "Sonja Henie," Christian said then. Christian's eyes caught the light from the southwest and turned as green as the glass of a broken Coke bottle.

"Forget it," Betty Lou advised her. Goldie agreed the past was irrelevant. "Besides," Betty Lou said, her chin squashed into a turkey wattle while she clenched the pillow with it and changed pillowcases, "if Dr. Turner said it was Monday, we'd know it was any day of the week but. He knows we know that. He's relying on it to upset you." Goldie nodded; the fact sufficed. She never argued with the way things were—only with the way they weren't. But persecution was not a member of the class of things amenable to analysis. It was simple, unpredictable, hard fact, the rough in the diamond, the thing you could never completely take into account in advance or dismiss afterward, the given, the doorway in the dark that transformed in a twinkling into a stranger with a knife. Evil was absurd; you couldn't dissect it like a frog, not even like the pregnant frog she'd carved open once, whose insides looked like a peanut butter-and-raisin sandwich. Its raisins had been tiny ones. She'd fallen into a reverie right in the laboratory, gazing so intently that the spots in the frog's belly became *muscae volitantes* and fogged her vision. Miles had whispered in her ear. He wasn't supposed to do that in class, but she liked him to. Nobody ever saw. The other girls had their heads down over their lab reports and failed to realize how serious things had gotten until Goldie told them she and Miles had set the date. It was the eighteenth of June. She wore laurel leaves and forget-me-nots in her hair, and a long white dress her sister had made for her. Miles was waiting at the altar. His curly hair had pins of light in it. She looked down the aisle, and the short aisle stretched into a vital journey; she was afraid she wouldn't be able to walk so far. Her father touched her on the back of her neck, as if she needed gentling, and he smiled at her and she at him. The pews on both sides surged with people. She was dizzy, the air was close, and one of the fans clacked along noisily at her back, like a lame horse. She was afraid something would happen to Miles before she could reach him, that he would vanish or be swept away in a pillar of cloud. But when she was halfway down the aisle he grinned, and she knew she was going to get there safely. She came up at his side, gasping a little, pitching slightly forward in step with her father, as if spurred on. The minister placed her hand in Miles's. It was well that he did that for her; she could not have done it herself, since her hand had gone as limp and clammy as a dead fish. Nevertheless, Miles seemed content to hold it, and when she looked at him, she understood how much he loved her and depended on her to be real.

SIX WORDS

Octopus loses arm, finds two legs.

SIX WORDS

Shark eats man, dies of hiccups.

WHEN WE ARRIVED IN THE DESERT

We'd have mistaken the desert for the end of the world were we not riding a slow-moving horse as nonchalant as, I don't know, Bing Crosby singing swing. Prickly saguaro look like a regiment of men who'd surrender rather than die. Fauna slink, slither, scrabble, crawl. Stars pin the sky to the ceiling.

BEGINNING AS OTHER

To begin as Other, that image without a reflection.

She dredged the lake of the mirror, finding every face but her own. At any time of month, her sleep was dreamless. Sometimes when she woke she remembered a color, a shape, a sound, but that was all—or no, not quite all, sometimes there was a taste on her tongue, bitter as blood. She felt a hunger she could not identify.

She woke hungering for something.

Woke to: the ferns speckled and shining with raindrops. A forest of ferns. A Siberian tiger with bike-spoke stripes radiating from his face like sun rays. The bear, huge and hidden. And the shy trilobite sinking into fossil.

Fins of a shark knifing the oceanic pie.

In the cave where she slept next to him, others curled into their own safe pockets, a ring of Others around a sleeping fire.

The fire dozed in its ashes.

Sometimes she almost remembered. She remembered someone,

something, had been hunting for her—no, hunting her. She remembered running, discovering the cave on the side of the hill.

The haven of the cave; the protection of his fortress body, his shielding arms.

She did not care for sex; she craved sex; she dreamed about it, couldn't keep from touching herself, thought sex was humiliating, thought sex was the body praising itself, thought sex was the heart synchronizing itself with history, thought sex was the only thing worth living for.

In one life, she taught school to students older than she, all boys (who would waste time and money educating a girl?). She was eighteen, and the students missed school so frequently for work on the farms that it was difficult for them to pass the standard examinations. But they would drive her into town, when she asked, for dry goods and groceries. They would give her an apple on the first day of class, a spiced orange at Christmas, a posy on the last day of the school year.

She imagined how one would love her so much that, loving her, he would become like Samson: strong, and a leader, but weak in the knees with devotion to his beloved.

She stopped dreaming about men. All the dreams were the same dream, and she had come to know it so well that she didn't have to bother to dream it. It was like knowing a joke by its number. "Dream #72," she would say to herself, and she would remember how it ended.

How it always ended: the reproaches, the phone calls that were supposed to inoculate against further phone calls but never did.

In one life, she moved to Paris and declared herself a lesbian. She wore a man's suit with a tailcoat and small-lensed reading spectacles and sturdy shoes with a bit of a heel. Men and women threw themselves at her feet, begging to be her lover. Everyone adores a lesbian, especially a cross-dressing lesbian, especially a cross-dressing lesbian in Paris.

The sounds of freight boats, their chugs and toots, carried into her apartment through the open window, the bleached muslin curtains shifting as if in response and making the diamonds of light on the white linoleum floor spin and dim and change places like a kaleidoscope. Sounds of automobiles, pedestrians, mounted police, a stray dog, children cross with tiredness (the long day, the demanding adults, the dancing classes and piano lessons, and endless waiting for parents to be done with whatever parents do), the pigeon on the sill, the starlings pouring themselves out of the darkening sky into a city tree, the tree outside her window.

In the bookstore with its used books with the oil of readers' palms rubbed deep into the covers, pages that seemed to have caught the breath of readers so that it flew out like a bird when the books were opened, she reached for a volume at the same time as Sandy (she would learn that was her name) and their fingers touched, then entwined. They fell in love and went to live in a rented villa where autumn's winds shuffled dry fallen leaves across the terrace. The leaves skirled even in through the open double door and piled up on the marble floor of the entryway. Sandy lay in bed upstairs, as if she were an invalid but she was not, writing passionate notes, on paper with grape vines in the margins!, to her other lovers. At dinner, Sandy sat thoughtfully staring at her, and she felt, beneath her lover's gaze, as if she were being compared, contrasted, reconsidered.

There was a war—when was there not? perhaps for a few years at most, here or there—and she escaped to it, disguising herself as a man, crossing borders, running guns and messages. Death piled up all around her like leaves, bonfires of death. She was ready to hurl herself onto one of the piles. She would not be missed. No one ever was, not for long.

As she started to throw herself forward, someone seized her by the waist and pulled her back, turned her toward him. Her face on his chest. Who was he? Did it matter? He was who was there, and she gave him everything she was and had been. She bore his child, a croupy, fearful boy with blue eyes and a gift for mathematics. He entered University at thirteen, was tenured at twenty.

Perhaps now she could forget about sex.

In her dreams she slept at the back of a cave, rock walls cool with moisture, or farther back, where the paintings were, none of herself, none of a woman, none of the animal that was woman. She woke to desire for something that did not exist. She woke to a world with grasses and seas and yet it was also a world that was lacking, there was something that did not exist that should have existed, something that was missing. She licked the sweat from the back of her hand and it tasted like blood.

♦ ♦ ♦

Fins of a shark, the ocean gold as the sun, the day circling like a shark.

The reclusive trilobite, which had never meant for anyone to know of its existence.

She got out of bed and snapped the shades up, brushed her teeth and dressed, drank coffee. Fetched the newspaper and slammed it down on the kitchen table! An aggrieved wife could kill a husband with a kitchen knife, pesticide, baling wire. Men were so mortal. The most complex man in the world was as biodegradable as grass.

Sometimes there was a taste on her tongue, blood as an appetizer, teasing her into desire. Was it her own blood? Had she been hunted down and left for dead? In the distance, cliffs dropped to the ocean like waterfalls, swift as wind shear. She could imagine herself falling into time, the downward arrow of narrative, the way all things work toward a punch line.

Yet even as she anticipates the end, new cities appear on the horizon—new empires. The future has arrived. In Newer New York, buildings float on glass foundations, the urban infrastructure repairs itself like a starfish growing a new arm, transportation is instantaneous. She works as an engineer in the sewers, keeping the system functional and efficient. Her hard yellow hat hangs on a peg in her locker. On the inside of the door of her locker she has hung photos of her husband, her children, her parents. She has hung a small mirror.

◆ ◆ ◆

Sometimes she has the night shift and is down here alone, under everything, beneath everything that is going on on top of the earth. It is like living in a cave, but when she sleeps the ocean glitters in her dreams with sunlit brightness; remembered glimmers of meadows and shining cliffs make her think, when she wakes, of—what? what was that she was dreaming, and what golden flame burned in her heart all night like autumn?

Of the generations who preceded her, of the ones to follow, she thinks: Time experiences itself as energy. To be alive is to feel alive.

Knows: We will miss nothing. Nothing is all there is.

The pipes clank and steam; a printout monitors the meters. Red tongues waggle within acceptable ranges on readouts. Ladders with narrow iron rungs climb up and down the levels.

HOW TO WRITE A STORY

A man and a woman. Opportunities for action abound. Let's say they are sitting on a blue sofa. Let's say he puts his arm around her. Let's say she lets it stay there but her posture remains stiff. Let's say he realizes this, gets up, says, "Did anyone ever tell you you're a cold fish?" He moves toward the door.

She says, "Yes."

"Yes?"

"Yes, I've been told that."

He walks back to the sofa and stands over her. "You're okay with that?"

"I can't help it."

"Of course you can."

"Well, I've never been able to."

He sits back down on the sofa. "For chrissake, just move closer. Here." He pulls his arm toward himself and her with it. She's still stiff. "Now relax," he says.

"I can't."

"You can."

"No, I—"

He grabs her by the shoulders and shakes her. Does he think she'll flop around, like a rag doll? Does he think he can make her lose her sense of propriety? Apparently so. "See?" he says. "Relaxed."

"I wouldn't say—"

"I know you wouldn't, but do you want to go through life being known as a cold fish?"

"No." The shaking had made her skirt ride up. She's wearing tiny earrings that look like buttons and she touches them to make sure they are still there. She wonders if he is going to beat her up. She should have just let him leave.

"Don't be scared," he says, as if he knows what she's thinking. "I just had to loosen you up. Are you always this uptight?"

"Yes."

He whistles through his teeth. "God, girl," he says. "Who or what terrified you into this condition?"

"I don't know. Nobody, really."

"Nobody. You're fooling yourself."

"Maybe. But I don't think so."

"Well, listen, he says, "just sit here while I—" He blows in her ear. She knows it should make her feel sexy but she just feels cold.

He kisses her neck, flicks at her earring with a finger. "Cute," he says.

She smiles, glad he likes the earrings. They are just like buttons on a shirt.

"Aha, a smile."

She ducks her head, afraid she is being made fun of.

Let's say he puts both arms around her and obliges her to face him. "Don't be shy," he says. "This is perfectly natural. You don't have to be afraid of me."

"I'm not."

"You sure act like you are."

"I'm not. I'm afraid of myself."

He moves back a few inches to stare her in the face. "Tell me," he says.

"I'm just afraid of what I might do if I lose control."

"What, you think you might kill me? What?"

"Nothing like that. But—"

He sees it now. She's afraid of orgasm. Of having an orgasm. "Oh, baby," he says, "it's just natural. You got to get that in your head."

"I know."

"Then just relax. Everything will work out."

"You think so?"

"I know so."

But it doesn't. It doesn't happen and he's fed up with her and she's depressed. So let's say she gets up from the bed and gets dressed in the same skirt and sweater she had on before and he lies there and watches her and says nothing. It's making her nervous, the nothing. But she warned him. She was honest. Why can't he be pleasant? Oh, of course—he feels like a failure. Men do. She's read about it. But still. She took all the blame in advance, so he should be able to be at least a little bit pleasant.

A man and a woman. So many things can happen between them. Maybe he's determined not to see her again or to keep seeing her until he conquers her. Maybe she never wants to see him again.

Or maybe they will work it out, become friends, live together, buy a cat, have a child. Then again, maybe when she heads to work in the morning she will be distracted, thinking over what has happened tonight, and fail to see the red light and the next thing you know sirens will be wailing, people will be running, police cars will be pulling up next to the bus. Between a man and a woman, anything can happen, including tragedy.

Tragedy happens all the time, so let's say she's dead. Dead to the world. When he tries to call her, no answer. When he tries to email her, no answer. When he tries to text her, no answer. He goes to her place, finds it locked, knocks on the supervisor's door, learns what happened.

He's not the kind of guy to see a psychoanalyst. It's either a bar or a church. You pick. Church it is. He goes to Confession and the priest tells him to do half-a-dozen Hail Marys. He does them and goes home, but at home he wants to go back to church. Or maybe to a bar. The thing is, her death is twisting his mind. He's got too much to think about now, what with the date and the only half-successful sex and now the death. It's like she's bewitched him or put a curse on him. Not that he believes in such things, he doesn't, but goddamn, it's what it fucking feels like.

I think you can take it from here.

LIFE

It's more than lively.

HE WASN'T THERE AGAIN TODAY

At Burnham and Burnham the coffee cart made rounds at ten and three and there were doughnuts and bagels as well as coffee. Robert had a habit of skipping breakfast, because he knew the coffee cart would come around. On Tuesday the sixteenth, it didn't.

He griped about it, but only to himself, at his cubicle near the far wall of the long room. It was his personal policy never to appear other than agreeable, a team player, and optimistic. This had stood him in good stead, or so he thought. He had been with Burnham and Burnham for twenty-two years.

The long room was divided into numerous cubicles, the walls of which rose four-and-a-half feet, so one could stand and look out at others who were standing. Standing, one could see the afternoon sun spilling through aluminum louvers. The building faced west.

After twenty-two years he'd become buddies with quite a few of his coworkers, male and female, but he lived alone. He had not planned to live alone. In fact, he'd always assumed he would marry and have kids, own a home; there would be a family dog, and a stray cat that they took in. His wife would want to work, of course, but she'd put the children's interests above her own. That this had not happened surprised him a little. When he tried to understand why it had not happened, he could think only that he hadn't found the right woman. Yet his friends had found wives. Sometimes he wondered if there was something wrong with him, some defect he was blind to while others were not. He smelled his tee-shirt before he pulled it on, making sure no armpit odor adhered. He wore clean underwear every day and changed it if he went out at night. He had drinks with friends but never drank alone. He didn't pick his teeth or his nose. His favorite car sticker was "Random Acts of Kindness." Was that a portrait of an unmarriageable man?

Had the firm decided against the coffee cart? Were Burnham and Burnham taking a cost-cutting measure?

He strolled through the long room, looking into cubicles. Some people had doughnuts. Some had bagels. Maybe they had bought them at kiosks and brought them to work. Maybe they had received a memo that someone had forgotten to give him.

His stomach was growling. He went out to lunch.

In the afternoon, the long room grew hot and sticky and the blinds had to be turned against the sun. But then it was too dark to read small fonts and people turned on their cubicle lamps, which were shaped like smaller versions of the aliens in the old *War of the Worlds*: an aluminum hood over a bulb atop a beastly neck that swiveled from the base.

The time was approaching three.

Robert waited in his cubicle for the cart's arrival. No cart came.

As he was leaving for the day, Robert asked Don, "How come there was no coffee cart today? Has it been cut from the budget?"

Don said, "What are you talking about? Of course there was a coffee cart today. You must have been away from your desk when it came by."

Had he been away from his desk and not realized it? He'd taken a stroll—everyone did that, they were encouraged to do that—

in lieu of an actual gym—but not during coffee-cart time. But maybe he'd been on the phone or computer and hadn't looked up at the right moment. But you could always hear the cart coming, the little wheels squeaking on the vinyl linoleum floor.

Robert's apartment was sparely furnished but comfortable. He had a La-Z-Boy in the living room in front of the TV. He ate off a TV table. Sometimes he thought about getting a decorator in—it would have to be a decorator, he didn't trust himself—but in the end he always decided there was no point in doing that. It wasn't as if he were besieged by guests. And he liked having dinner in front of the nightly news.

His bedroom was more welcoming: a double bed with down comforter, willow oak on view out the window. The ceiling was light blue and the walls were an unworrisome beige. A restful room, and yet cheerful, too, because of the window and the willow oak.

The coffee cart failed to stop at his cubicle on Wednesday as well. If it had rolled by anybody's cubicle. He stepped outside to look and could spot no coffee cart.

But when he went for his stroll—which had practically been mandated by Burnham and Burnham—there were crumbs on desks and people holding Styrofoam cups. He made a detour to his supervisor but stopped outside the office. Did he want to sound like a spoiled child? Did he want his supervisor to think he had nothing better to do than complain? No. He turned back toward his cubicle. Don brushed by him without speaking. Robert turned around and saw that Don was moving swiftly down the hallway. No doubt he had something urgent on his mind, Robert thought. Or maybe he was in a hurry to the Men's Room. Maybe, he thought, someone had baked a laxative into the doughnuts and bagels and he should be grateful the coffee cart had not come by his cubicle. He smiled a grim smile.

Jody knocked on the frame of his cubicle to ask if he'd like to join a group going out for lunch. "Indian," she said. "A buffet. They have Tandoori."

Jody looked good posing in the doorless frame. She was married to a man named Burt who worked somewhere else. He glanced at her wedding band. "No thanks," he said. "I think I'd better work through lunch."

"Okay, then," she said. "We'll miss you." Her voice was slightly sandpapery. He liked it. After she left, he thought for a moment about how much he liked it. Then he turned to his work. There was never a day when there was no work to turn to.

He tried to catch Don's eye when the closing bell rang but somehow he couldn't. He'd thought he might casually mention Jody and see if Don said anything about her marriage. Don was walking out with someone else and rushed right by him again.

Robert hoped Jody would drop by again on Thursday but of course she didn't. People didn't eat Indian every day of the week. Well, in India they did, but not here. Which made him think of the coffee cart. Once again, he was left out. He decided he *would* complain to the supervisor. He could do it in a friendly way, maybe ask if someone new was pushing the cart and didn't realize there were cubicles in the back of the room. Though his cubicle was the only cubicle in the back.

He knocked on his supervisor's door and waited. And waited.

"I don't know, man," Ed said, from his cubicle next to the supervisor's office. "He was just there. I didn't see him go out."

As Robert moved away from the office he saw Jody walk up to it. Saw her knock, saw the door open, saw her go in. Was Jody having an affair with their supervisor? She wouldn't be complaining about the coffee cart. He'd seen the half-chewed bagel on her keyboard.

Pictures of Jody and the supervisor behind a closed door flickered in his mind, something like a poorly made porn video in which you could never really see the faces or the parts.

He walked back to the supervisor's office. If sex was going on in there, they would just have to stop. He knocked, then knocked again. Then he knocked some more. He looked over at Ed's cubicle but if Ed was in it, he wasn't coming out, any more than Jody or the supervisor. And even if they were in the throes, wouldn't the knocking make them stop? He stopped knocking and put his ear to the door. Nothing. He couldn't hear anything. Wait—that was a gasp, he was sure it was a gasp. Followed by a sandpapery giggle.

He went to the Men's Room and stayed a while for the quiet. When he came out it was so close to quitting time that instead of going back to his office he took an elevator to the lobby and left the building.

How could they not have heard him, he wondered. They must have heard his knocking. They must have thought as long as they didn't open the door, they wouldn't be found out. If he knew where Burt worked, he thought, he might have gone to tell him that his wife was cheating on him. No, he wouldn't, he thought. He'd never say anything like that to anyone.

He took off his clothes and crawled under the comforter, though the comforter was not really necessary this time of year. He didn't eat; he didn't feel like eating, or TV.

He wanted to fall asleep so the video in his head would stop playing and after awhile it did slow down and he dozed lightly. He dreamed the coffee cart stopped at his cubicle and that it held not only doughnuts and bagels but creampuffs and cupcakes. He hated cupcakes and couldn't account for their presence in his dream. There was latte along with the coffee. He tried to see who was pushing the cart but couldn't. He could smell the coffee, though. It was dark and aromatic, like chocolate. When he thought of chocolate in his dream, he saw the ice cream sandwiches of his youth, with their chocolate cookie coverings frontside and back. Then he was in a pool like the one at the YMCA where his parents had taken him after his bout with rheumatic fever. The doctor had advised them that walking in a pool would strengthen his muscles. The water had been so warm, warmer than it usually is in pools. He woke up and threw off the comforter, which had overheated him.

Friday he slung his jacket onto the coat stand before sitting down at his desk. He'd been reviewing spread sheets for an hour when he heard Ed and Don at the entrance to his cubicle, which was so far in the back that visitors were rare. That was one reason the coffee cart had been so meaningful to him: a visit from a human being twice a day.

But now Ed and Don, talking loudly, were entering his cubicle. Their arms were full of boxes; Don's chin rested on papers atop the top box. He set his boxes down in a corner and said, "I've been sent to Siberia. It's a demotion."

"Nonsense," Ed said. "Look how much bigger this cubicle is than either of ours. You're getting it because they think you need the space. It's a bonus."

From the first box Don removed framed photographs that he placed on Robert's desk. Don with his wife and daughter. His daughter when she was young, posing with two kittens. A close-up of his wife's face, smiling and with her hair blowing in the wind (also, Robert thought, taken long ago). Don next to his Nissan Sentra.

Robert couldn't help but notice that the photographs transformed the space. The cubicle looked cozier, friendlier. Ed pulled out from under his arm two large pictures and from his shirt pocket a small packet of stick-on hooks; he stuck a couple of the hooks on the short wall to accommodate the two large pictures, and now Robert's cubicle looked like a real room. One picture was an enlarged photo Don had taken in England, of the Thames in Cambridge, surrounded by autumn trees. Don had once invited Robert into his former cubicle to view it. The other, new to Robert, was a charcoal portrait. "My wife," Don said to Ed, "by my daughter." Robert thought it was very good. He said so to Don, but Don ignored him.

Robert tugged at Don's sleeve but again, Don ignored him.

A thought occurred to Robert, but not like a light bulb turning on. It would be more accurate to say that it broke over Robert's head like dawn, a slow sunrise. As his thought became clear to Robert he began to sweat. His armpits, his hands. His face. He wondered if he smelled.

"She's talented," Ed said. "Of course I understand zilch about art."

Don leaned against the desk. "What do you suppose happened to Robert?"

"Who knows," Don said. "Maybe he just got tired of showing up."

"I worry about him. Poor bastard."

"Well, there's nothing anyone can do. Enjoy your new crib." Ed slapped Don on the back and left. Don, still standing, gazed at the pictures on the wall. They reassured him against the idea of demotion. Family pictures will do that, will establish a man's reality, for himself and for others. He did need more space. Brightening, he flung himself into the chair that Robert had thought he was occupying. But Robert was not in the chair, nor anywhere else. If I were in the chair, Robert said to himself, then Don would be elsewhere, and if Don is in the chair, I am not. Logic couldn't be any clearer than that. He tried to shout—to Don, to anybody—but although a page of one of the spread sheets stirred slightly, as if lifted by a breeze, there was no sound.

ON TEACHING

It was a nice day so I joined my kids on the playground. Shadows made the small cotton-ball clouds look scruffy, as if they were children with dirt on their faces. They needed to be scrubbed with a damp washrag. Children, children, I said twice, clapping smartly each time. They circled me. They surrounded me. I was shaken to see that they were drawing the circle tighter and I had become their prisoner. How had this happened? I was going to clap a third time but one of the children shushed me with a finger over her lips. I felt, I felt—outraged. Who were they to dictate to me? The teacher was I. The leader was I. They were the helpless children. Surely that's right. Surely that's how it's always been. Is this a trick? A prank? Children have a habit of playing pranks, don't they. A prank, then. A silly—

"Mrs. Morgan," the girl who dared to shush me said.

"Yes. What is happening here?"

"Happening?"

"What is going on here?"

"Going on?"

They came closer and closer, the circle closing, their shoes scuffing mine, their sweetish breath—breaths—making my heart beat faster, making it hard for *me* to breathe.

> *One-love, two-love, three-love, four.*
> *See the teacher on the floor.*

One of them had tripped me, and though I wasn't on the floor I was indeed lying on the ground, one of my shoes beside my hip.

> *Five-love, six-love, seven-love, eight.*
> *See the teacher take the bait.*

What the hell did that mean? Their chanting made me frantic. I stood up, holding the shoe that came off. With one shoe on and one off I had to shift from side to side.

> *Nine-love, ten-love, eleven-love, twelve.*
> *Here's a book you really should shelve.*

They are telling me I should go shelve a book! Who do they think they are?

> *One-love, two-love, three-love, four.*
> *Take yourself thence and come no more.*

Because I had one foot in a shoe and the other in only a sock, I had to bob up on one leg and sink down on the other. They had stripped me of my dignity. "What do you want?" I asked.

"Take yourself thence and come no more," they said as one.

At my desk in the schoolroom I wrote a letter of resignation and signed it with my good ballpoint. I handed in grades—all A's, because I was afraid they might retaliate if I failed them. I cleaned out my desk drawers. I did feel a bit sad when I did that but the sadness didn't last long.

BURNING THE BABY

Someone struck a match and the baby went up in flames. Members of the family choked on the sickening smell. The father was afraid to look at the mother: surely she would not have done this to her own child. Yet he remembered when his son, sixteen, slapped her in the face and she screamed at him, *Edward, hit him, hit him.* He could not bring himself to hit his son and she never forgave him for that. The mother looked at the father quickly, then looked down at the floor. He would not have done such a thing, would he? But the baby was burnt, there was no question about that. Sweet little babe, now blackened and flaking, now something like a tiny Christmas tree charred by lightning. The older brother made measurements, seeking to determine how much shorter the baby was post-burning. The baby's legs, roly-poly and chubby, were burnt off at the knees, which meant it could not even crawl. Of course, being dead meant that too. The sister tried to comb the baby's burnt hair but it fell out in bunches. The sister began to cry. The baby wouldn't crawl or play with her. Had the sister done something wrong? What had she done? What? She tickled the baby but it still refused to laugh or squeal. She was in trouble, she knew. She was supposed to watch out for her baby sister, keep her happy, make sure no harm came to her. No harm! She wanted to die. She thought her parents probably wanted her to die. She didn't dare look at them. They would be so angry with her.

THE DOORBELL

The doorbell is ringing. She ignores it, thinking whoever it is will come again and not when she's so busy. She is busy cleaning papers from her desk, putting them in order. The desk is in her upstairs office, where the cat likes to stretch out on the braided rug. Who would be calling at the house this early in the morning? No one she knows. The cat yawns silently and rolls over on the rug. The papers—how did she acquire so many papers? Should she save them for a library? But no one has asked for her papers. Rough drafts, mostly. She is a lady who scribbles. Why is that so much more pathetic than a man who scribbles? Oh: the man writes, the lady scribbles. She tosses a full file folder into the trash basket. The cat, annoyed by this disturbance, jumps onto the armchair, curls up, and goes back to sleep. Who could have been ringing the doorbell? Quit thinking about it, it wasn't important. Most of the time, nothing is important. Birth, death, love are important, that's about it. Not a doorbell. The sun does something balletic—a glissando across the room—and she retrieves the file from the trash basket, thinking maybe she should hang on to it, you never know. Someone might want her papers after all. The cat rolls over in the armchair and the tiny bell on his collar tinkles. Sometimes the cat tries to play with the bell but he can't reach it and always gives up quickly. The sun lies down on the braided rug as if for a long rest. Her grandmother gave her that rug many years ago. Her grandmother has been dead for a long time and to tell the truth, she doesn't really remember her all that well. The doorbell rings. She stops what she is doing to listen to it ring. Who can it be? She listens as it continues to ring.

ABEBE

A boy in Africa has a distended stomach. Or rather, many boys in Africa have a distended stomach. This boy is named Abebe. He lies on a cot. His grandfather leans over the cot to stroke his grandson's hair back from his sweaty forehead. Abebe does not cry, nor can he talk. Breathing takes all of his energy. He wheezes like a hundred-year-old man. His skin is black but his face is pale, like old ashes. His eyes are as dry as sandpaper. His legs are weak and somewhat bowed. In fact, his thighs are barely able to support his body. There *are* tears in his grandfather's eyes, and his grandfather's tears course down his face. Various sores have infested the boy's skin. Some are bloody. The grandfather presses gauze onto the bleeders and the gauze sticks. Abebe gasps, choking on air. He is in a room with slow-moving ceiling fans and mosquito netting. The grandfather was able to arrange those things.

Abebe knows that most starving boys do not have cots, ceiling fans, netting, or even a grandfather. He is glad to have them but he doesn't believe they will help. Maybe it helps to have his grandfather here, but what can he do? Not much, Abebe thinks.

Abebe's grandfather knows full well that what he has accomplished is not sufficient unto the day but he can't tell that to Abebe.

Abebe's grandfather drove a taxi in Minnesota. He tried to get Abebe's parents to cross the ocean just as he had but they would not leave their home. They were murdered by rebels. Now there is no home. No home and no parents. Only a grandfather. Who is kind and worried but cannot save his grandson. Abebe is sure of this.

Abebe is ten, but he looks six. When he remembers his parents he wants to cry, though, as you know, he can't, not now. His father was a herder. His mother took in washing. Abebe had wanted a brother or a sister to play with but a doctor told his mother she could not have any more children.

Abebe's grandfather is holding Abebe's hand but he is afraid to squeeze it. He worries that he would break Abebe's finger bones if he did. When Abebe dies, it will be the end of his line. There is no other child to carry on.

The ceiling fan sometimes stirs the netting and then the netting brushes Abebe's ashen face.

If only I had heard earlier! the grandfather thinks. He sends up quick prayers for his grandson—silently, because he doesn't want to alarm him.

Abebe wishes his grandfather could tell him how long this will last, this dying. He hurts. His chest, his stomach, his legs hurt.

Grandfather kisses Abebe's forehead and tells him he'll be back in a second.

Abebe watches the shadow the fan throws on the wall.

Grandfather returns with a doctor. "He will give you an injection to make you feel better, Abebe."

In Abebe's opinion, no injection ever makes anyone feel better. Needles hurt! But this sentence is too long for him to get it out.

The needle goes into his arm and of course it hurts. "You'll feel better soon," Grandfather says.

The doctor nods. "That's right, son," he says.

A tear appears in Abebe's eye. The right eye.

It stands there in his eye. It doesn't fall.

"Now, now," Grandfather says. "You'll feel better in just a minute."

And miraculously, Abebe thinks he feels a little better. The leg pains are easing, especially the pain at the top of his legs, where the buttocks begin. His various sores become less irritating. He stops thinking about them altogether. He can hardly believe it: the pain is being chased from his body. He thinks of the swimming hole where he and his friends hung out. He can almost smell his mother's cooking. He remembers the clapboard school he went to, and the nuns who taught him how to draw and read and multiply.

Grandfather is crying again. He wants to tell him he can stop now. All the pain is going away.

SIX WORDS

Morning to night: a daily adventure.

SIX WORDS

Night to morning: the courageous return.

WHEN WE ARRIVED AT THE MOUNTAIN

We hadn't known it would stretch from earth to the sky, though we should have anticipated that. The peak punctured heaven. Or would have, if there were a heaven. Snow crystallized from the cold air. Geysers froze. Frost bit our fingers. We saw the world in stasis, hushed, balanced on the diving board.

THE PRESIDENT OF NO PLACE
IN PARTICULAR

The president of no place in particular is lost. He cannot find his office. He wanders streets at night, opens doors by day, but still he cannot find no place in particular. Indeed, he sees that everywhere there is a place in particular. He thinks: *Maybe I'm not president of anything.* Then thinks again: *But I hold the title. I was elected.*

By whom? Who elected him?

The citizens, of course. They cast their votes. The votes were counted. He won.

Won what?

The right to rule the country for four years, assuming no one impeached him.

Yes, yes, he thinks. *All that is correct. But this country is too big. This country called no place in particular.*

Maybe he should call himself the president of America in general.

Hmm. That sounds good. As president of America in general his office could be anywhere. Or everywhere. He would no longer be lost, wandering the streets. The citizens would know where to find him. Why, he would be wherever he was!

Sounds like a plan, he thought.

He changed his title to president of America in general. It was almost as hard as being the president of no place in particular, but at least he had an office and could go there.

MUSTAFA ENTERS FIRST GRADE

He is five, starting first grade half a year early. He has two new pencils, a pack of crayons, an eraser that crumbles when he erases, and new shoes. He can already read; he taught himself at the age of three. He is eager, excited, and scared. Will the kids like him? Will the teacher? If the kids don't like him, he plans to beat them up. Just because he knows how to read doesn't mean he's a sissy. But his mothers told him to be polite to everyone—the kids, the teachers, the janitor. They are all important people, he was told.

He has two mothers. Most families have one mother and one father, or only one mother. His mothers told him that. Mom Licia (for Alicia) stays at home to paint pictures. Mom Jill goes to work, where she makes money writing ads. He has seen ads in newspapers and on TV, so he has a sense of what she does. He does not want to paint pictures or write ads. He wants to be a fireman. He has a play fireman hat and wears it often at home but his mothers won't let him wear it today. They brush his short hair, tuck his shirt into his jeans, and hand him a small case that includes the pencils, the crayons, and the eraser, and to his delight, a small plastic ruler.

It is early September, a coolness in the air that makes him feel sort of bubbly. He skips beside Mom Jill to the sedan. She opens the passenger door and he scrambles in. When she gets behind the wheel she smiles at him. "First grade!" she says, like an announcement. "You're a big boy now."

He puffs up his chest as much as he can and punches the air with his fist.

At school, he has to stand up, state his first name, and say one thing about his summer. "Mustafa," he says. "I read a book called *The Black Stallion*."

"You mean somebody read it to you."

"No, ma'am, I read it."

The little girl next to him had crawled under her chair to hide, although everyone could see her. She looked up at Mustafa with a finger over her lips, saying "Shh."

"I taught myself," he said.

The teacher told him to go to the Principal's office. She didn't tell him where that was, so he sat down on a bench in the hall. But that got boring fast, so he opened a door that had "LIBRARY" on it. He was the only person there and yet so many books beckoned to him. He focused on the shelves he could reach. Many were picture books, like *Goodnight Moon*, which Mom Licia had read to him. He still liked to think about that book. He found *The Blue Truck*: that was fun, and he thought about reading it out loud to the other first graders. He took it off the shelf and went back to the classroom. Everyone looked up when he walked in.

"Did you go to the Principal's office, Mustafa?"

The teacher obviously didn't trust him.

"No, ma'am—" he began.

The teacher told the student teacher to keep the class quiet. She seized Mustafa's hand and marched him to the Principal. She explained the problem to the Principal. The Principal invited Mustafa to sit down.

Mustafa noticed that she had gray curls. She wore a gray dress and a gray cardigan. Why did old people wear gray? Maybe they just *felt* gray, he thought. "You've read *The Black Stallion*?"

"Yes, ma'am."

"Can you tell me about it?"

Mustafa launched into a detailed telling of the story.

"Your parents didn't read it to you?"

"They don't need to read to me now. But sometimes I wish they still would."

"What's that in your hand?"

"*The Blue Truck*, ma'am. I would like to read it to the other kids. It's a simple book but it's fun. They will like it."

The gray principal looked at the now red-faced teacher. "I'm sure they will."

The teacher smiled, a sickly kind of smile, but she took Mustafa back to the class and allowed him to read *The Blue Truck* to his classmates.

None of them would ever not like him.

It was Licia who picked him up because Mom Jill was still at work. "How did it go? Your first day?"

"Just fine, Mom."

"Did you have fun?"

"Sure."

"Did you learn anything?

Did he learn anything? He had to think about that. "Maybe," he said.

"Maybe?"

"I think maybe the teacher learned more than I did."

His mom gave him a sharp look. Then she said, "I wouldn't be surprised."

ACCIDENTS OF THE SOUL
IN OUR DAY AND AGE

You may have noticed that things have changed since the Middle Ages. Back then, "the accident of the soul" was a doctrine similar to the Roman Catholic idea of original sin: we carried with us the sin of Adam's flagrancy, his disobedience to God. The Orthodox Church, for one, promulgated this piece of wisdom. Even the purest being on the planet had inherited death from Adam, and there was no way to cleanse that spot of sin on the soul. It was an "accident" because no one could avoid being born, and being born meant being born after Adam, his sin in our genes, although the thought was that we "contracted" his sin though we might not commit it.

Nowadays a soul might ride up on the curb, whereas in the Middle Ages it would have found itself stretched on the rack. The soul that was burned alive now simply stumbles on the sidewalk. Torn souls used to require a ripping apart in order to stitch back together, but now a 3-D printer can whip up a replacement in no time.

Still, some things remain the same. The soul that fell down the stairs is in a cast—has been ever since, and likely to be so for some time. The soul that took a slug from a cop's gun died the next day. I know a soul who broke a leg doing wheelies in the woods. And oh yes, there was a soul that managed to drown. Souls shouldn't drown. They are meant to rise to ethereal regions where cherubim catch hold of them like balloons and escort them to the angels, who would take care of them forever. But that drowned soul had got entwined with underwater weeds and, with each attempt to pull free, sank more deeply into the muck and mire.

Still again, most souls find their way to heaven. Unfortunately, in our day and age, there are those who would dispatch souls to the higher world long before their time is come. Al-Qaeda, Al-Shabaab, Boko Haram, Al-Qaeda in the Arabian Peninsula (AQAP), ISIL, Assad—but of course to meet up with such as these is not an accident so much as it is murder, and as the subject of my piece was accidents of the soul, not murders of the same, so shall I put an end to it right here.

SENIORS AT THE MOVIE

Hey, isn't that the guy who was in?

That movie called?

That's it. He's married to?

How would I know who he's married to? That's your department.

My department! Aren't you a married man? I believe I'm your wife!

I don't care who's married to whom. Not when it comes to movie stars, anyway.

But you care about who's acting in what.

That's different. That has a relation to what we choose to watch.

Maybe. Maybe not.

What the hell does that mean? You know it does.

I just wanted to know if he was the guy in that movie we saw.

We must have seen hundreds of movies.

Thousands. Millions.

No, we haven't seen millions.

It feels like it, though.

Look! That's—what's her name?

It sure is.

She's a good actor.

I agree.

But what's her name? Tillie? Terry? Tootsie?

You're thinking of Jessica Lange. It's not Jessica Lange.

Jessica Lange was gorgeous, though.

She was. Not now.

She's still a good actor.

Have you seen her in anything lately?

'Fraid not.

She was doing those horror shows.

I didn't realize that.

Well, I don't like horror, so we didn't go.

Do you remember. . . .What was the name of that movie?

Where she was kind of flaky?

Yeah. She was so good in that.

Blue skies? Something like that?

Blue Sky.

That's right. And that wasn't the only—

Frances. The one about Frances Farmer.

We saw her do Blanche DuBois. Was that in New York or London?

I don't recall.

But you remember we saw her.

Yes. Darling, I do not have Old Timer's.

You mean Alzheimer's.

Whatever.

Do you know she's no longer with what's his name? Sam something?

Really? I thought that was forever.

So you do care about who's married to whom.

I'm sorry the marriage didn't last. It looked like they were good together.

Marriage is hard.

Are you talking about us?

Well, you have to admit it's hard. You don't always like me.

But I always love you. Like is different.

I'd say I like you.

Not love?

Sometimes.

Sweetie, you don't always like me, either.

That's your narcissism.

I am not a fucking narcissist!

Shush.

Don't shush me.

Okay. I'm not shushing you.

Thank you. Jesus.

Why do we even *go* to the movies?

Because we like stories.

That's true. May I have some more popcorn?

He pours more popcorn into her small plastic tray.

I hate this stuff.

I love it.

It's kind of sickening. I wish they could serve us what? Anything but popcorn.

Steak. I'd like a steak.

That guy! He was in *Downton Abbey.*

You're right. It's him all right. Nice to see him in a movie role.

He's gotten stockier.

A little.

Well, I'm glad we figured that out.

But what about Jessica Lange?

What about her?

She's divorced. That can't be good.

She's strong. She'll survive.

Maybe so.

I wouldn't.

You wouldn't?

Promise you will never divorce me.

I think I already made that promise.

Promise me again.

Okay, I promise.

THE DISH

He was so good-looking she thought she might drool on him if
he came any closer. He came closer. He pressed his lips to hers
and she thought how nice it would be to stay like that, mouth on
mouth, for a few centuries. For millennia. Then her husband
shook her by the shoulder. "Wake up! You're talking in your
sleep," he said.

THE DEPARTMENT OF MIRTH
AND LAUGHTER

We are located in Paris, on the right side of the Left Bank. Where else? Where else is there so much bubbly, so much discreetly beautiful light that falls on roofs and the Seine, Notre Dame and sidewalk cafés?

To obtain your license for unlicensed behavior, you must apply in person. Please note: while the Department is generally inclined toward inclusivity, not everyone is welcome. Cynics, for example. We grant no permits to cynics. One more thing to be cognizant of: mirth and laughter are not the same thing. Mirth is an attitude; laughter is an activity.

Upon entering the building, look to the left. You will see a door with an upper pane of frosted glass. The pane bears a pink tinge so you will enjoy a rosy view of it.

Knock. Maybe no one will answer. If so, that is because the staff is busy laughing. Knock again.

Someone will open, eventually. You will find yourself in a storeroom with racks of champagne, shelves of toys, displays of rollicking clowns. If a hand lifts your skirt just a tad, do not be offended too quickly: flirting is *de rigueur* here. But only flirting. Talk should not be too blue.

There are chocolates and candies, including lemon drops. There are pastries, especially croissants and sweet crêpes. Such tidy edibles are known to increase pleasure.

Immediately upon receipt of your license, handsome Frenchmen will kiss the back of your hand, tell you how gorgeous you are. They do this whether you are gorgeous or not. They do it because you have your license to licentious behavior. Also because they are Frenchmen. (Switch the sexes if you are male, if you want to switch them.)

In other rooms there are sofas and lounges, silk pillows, cool linen sheets. Everyone is laughing. Everyone is having a good time.

Do not expect card games, video games, or roulette. We find that our licensees become addicted to them, which takes all the fun out. For similar reasons, we allow no Internet access.

But the Department can make available yo-yos, Etch A Sketch tablets, watercolors, and rose petals to sprinkle on the cool linens. We also offer Slinkys and Shmoom, as they are among the biggest laugh-getters.

We are always delighted by how a light heart will lead to romance. And almost always it does.

Smoking is not allowed, not even for French philosophers.

There is no limit to how long you may stay. Time is limitless when one is having a *good* time.

Whenever you do choose to leave, we will present you with the small gift of a box of Merrimints. They are delicious, tingling, and life-affirming.

ON BALLOONS

It's the air in the o's that allow the balloon to fly.

JUST SAYIN'

People love people who love people.

DEREK

She named him Derek. It was the name that came to her, for no reason she could think of, and it had all the more urgency for having no reason. The name seemed to fit him. His mother had abandoned him. Mother bats often leave their babies behind; something frightens them and they save themselves before they stop to think about the baby. (There's usually only one baby at a time; occasionally there are twins.) Or she may have died, perhaps in a heat wave, which can kill off huge numbers of bats.

She found Derek when she was digging out weeds next to the barn. She called a wildlife shelter to ask what to do. "Don't touch it. Bring it in," they said, and she did, but she had already touched it. In the shelter was a long row of bat babies, each one swaddled in a knitted scarf or dish cloth. Their wings were under these wraps. The darling creatures looked like little bat burritos—that is what they are called. Or one could say they resembled corn husks. To see a bat fly out of a chimney or across the moon can be scary: the bats are swift and their wings relatively huge. But tucked into their scarves, with their wings folded and only the little heads peeking out, they look like sweet, snuggly, sleepy babies.

She held Derek, wrapped up, in her hands, presenting him to the shelter workers.

"Derek?" they said. "Is he male?"

She didn't know. It hadn't occurred to her that he might be female.

They lifted him up for examination.

"He's no Debbie," they said, "so you're in luck."

A shelter worker was rubbing Derek gently on his stomach, though such a tiny stomach could only be a tummy. Then the worker picked up an eyedropper and squeezed some milk into his mouth. "You know they can carry rabies?" the worker asked.

"Yes," she said, thinking, *Derek doesn't have rabies.*

"Derek doesn't have rabies," said the worker, then added, "They're called pups."

"The babies, not the rabies, I assume." She smiled.

The worker looked at her as if she might be mentally challenged.

"He's falling asleep."

"Pups do that. Especially when they've sipped enough milk. They are, after all, mammals."

I knew that, she wanted to say. "Why are some of the others squeaking?"

"All bat pups have to practice echolocation. They have different calls and have to figure out which are theirs. They also have to learn to fly, just as birds do."

"Is there anything else you can tell me?" She hadn't known that bats had different methods of echolocation.

"Ever seen a microbat?"

She shrugged, not knowing whether she had or hadn't.

"There's a bumblebee bat."

"That's very alliterative."

"Allit—? Sure. The bumblebee bat is *maybe* the size of a jellybean." The worker glanced away from Derek and looked straight into her eyes. "It weighs about as much as a penny weighs. Actually, it weighs a little less than that."

She stared back at the worker. "May I take Derek home now?"

"He's probably better off here."

"But I found him."

"And you brought him here, where you knew he would be better off."

"But he belongs to me." Her voice was rising, and she tried to quell her fears.

"Bats are wildlife. They don't belong to anybody. I'm sure you can understand that."

"It's not a question of understanding. The fact is that Derek is mine. I found him."

"Maybe I'd better get my boss. She can explain it to you better than—"

"There's nothing to explain. Just give me back my bat."

"I can't!"

She swooped Derek up and put him in her shirt pocket. A little guano didn't worry her.

The worker ran after her, shouting Stop! Stop!

Why would she stop? Derek was *her* baby. Nobody could tell her otherwise.

MUNICIPAL

They raised fortifications, making natural use of a river that ran nearby, and brought their wives and children to live in houses with shaded entrances. The sky opened up, giving chimneys and roofs elbow room. A wall that had once protected the city from invaders crumbled, and now weeds and vines knitted the bricks together. The river was like theme music, repeating itself at different speeds, fast in some places, slow in others. When it rained, the populace stayed indoors, or strolled about holding umbrellas, or dashed from dark, dripping doorway to dark, dripping doorway with newspaper tenting their heads. More winters came, and more blue-skyed summers, and finally the original fortifications, including the Old Wall, could be traced only on maps in museums or the city surveyor's office. The New People plunk down hard-earned cash to receive lapel pins that let them walk through rooms overflowing with artifacts. They take tour buses to churches and cemeteries. The original people's names, carved into stone, seem almost like a foreign tongue because hardly anyone names their children with those names anymore, as is true, for example, of a tour group that arrives on a bright, windy day, among whose number are Luz, Brasch, and Zave. On the other hand, wildflowers retain their former names, and, on this bright, windy day, Smartweed, Loosestrife, Lobelia, and Gentian tremble, as if frightened, and cast their moving shadows over the tombstones so that the carved letters dance a little; and the river is still playing its song.

SIX WORDS

Sun dies out. So do we.

VASILY VASILYEVICH SLIVOWITZ

Vasily Vasilyevich was lying vacant-minded in his coffin when his cell phone rang. He had not realized he had his cell with him. Or that he was in his coffin. His wife must have slipped the phone into his trouser pocket when the funeral people weren't looking. "Sveta?" he asked. He bumped his head when he tried to sit up and was now rubbing it.

"Da," she said.

"You shouldn't be talking to me, Sweetums. I'm dead."

"God, don't I know it. But we have unfinished business."

Unfinished business? He was puzzled, since he himself was plainly finished.

"Vasilich, dear, you died without paying the heating bill."

"Doesn't our beloved Russian Federation pay for our heat?" It was always best to preface the RF with *beloved*. Putin could get very angry when there was no *beloved*.

"Also, little Boris has outgrown his coat with the furry hood. He needs new one."

"Already?"

"Kids grow," Sveta said.

"So fast?"

"Yes so fast."

"What do you expect me to do about it?"

"Can't you, I don't know, call in a loan?"

"My being dead must have addled your mind. We've never had a loan to call in. Don't you remember that we were always the ones who owed?"

Sveta sighed. "I thought maybe things would be different now."

"Well, they certainly are for me." Vasily's nose was itching. He scratched it, and that made him sneeze.

"You sound just the same, Vasilich. Scratching and sneezing."

What she didn't know was that his balls were itching too. He tried to settle them but there wasn't much room in his coffin. It wouldn't surprise him if the RF had made coffins smaller to save money. Not that Putin was short on money. Heavens, no. Putin was so fucking rich he could buy and sell King Midas. "Sweetums, you'll have to find a way to pay the heating bill yourself, Sweetums." Two Sweetums.

Sweetums began to cry. Little snifflings at first, and then they got bigger and louder.

"Stop crying, Sweetums. Please."

"I need you to come home and tend to things. I can't do it by myself." Her voice began to rise again, not louder but higher.

"Dear Sveta, I'm in a coffin. You may remember—"

"You've had a nice rest, Vasilich. Now come home."

"I can't get out of this coffin."

"You have muscles, Vasilich. Many more muscles than I have. Punch the top."

"Punch the top?" He thought for a while. Then he balled his fists and punched the top of his coffin. Sure enough, it fell apart. He should have known that a Russian coffin would be no problem to break out of. Nothing in Russia was well made unless it was made for an oligarch. "It worked!"

"Of course it worked. This country is shit."

"But there's a ton of dirt on top of me."

"I doubt it," said Sveta.

So he started digging with his hands. Clods of dirt rained on his head. Turnips fell on him. Carrots. Beets. He filled his pockets with the beets; they would make a good borscht. And—before he knew it, he was topside.

"I'm out, Sveta."

"I knew it. There are so many dead Russians that the only way to bury them is on top of one another."

"You are right, Sveta. I concede."

"So. Now you can come home."

"It's true I'm out of the grave, but I'm still dead." He sat down next to a tombstone. "I'm still dead," he said again.

"Are you talking to me?" Sveta said, rather like Robert De Niro.

"I believe so."

"Are birds singing?"

"Even in a graveyard."

"Are you hungry?"

He thought of the beets stuffed in his pockets. He thought how comfortingly warm the soup would be when it was in his stomach, how delicious it would be with cold vodka. "Yes," he said.

"Then even if you are dead, you are as good as alive. Come home."

So he walked out of the cemetery and when he got to his house, Sveta was waiting for him. "You need to let me wash the dirt out of your hair," she said, leading him to the kitchen sink. There was no sink in the bathroom.

Vasily let her bend his head over the basin. It was good to feel her fingers in his hair again. It made him nostalgic and calm and a little bit hard. Could a dead man have sex? he wondered.

"When your hair is clean and the heating bill is paid," Sveta said, reading his mind.

Well, that gave him something to look forward to!

"But we have no way to pay the bill," he said.

"You'll have to go back to work."

"Work? But I'm sure I've already been struck from the work list! They like their workers to be alive. Or at least only half-dead."

"You can change your name. They'll never know it's you."

"But I look like me!"

"Honey Pie," Sveta said, "you no longer look like you. You look dignified, older, and serious."

"Death did that to me?"

"Da. In spades."

"I guess death is not a joking matter. Death makes a man think seriously about things. By the way—" He pulled the beets from his pockets. "I picked these for a borscht."

"I'll start it as soon as you go to the plant." She finished drying his hair with a towel.

"Suppose they recognize me? They'll think I'm trying to work double time."

"No they won't. You forget the former you is dead."

"So is the latter me."

"They won't know that."

Vasily went to the plant and they gave him a job. He was to insert ignitions into automobiles. Tedious, but not difficult. When he returned home, the borscht was waiting on the stove. The smell of it was so splendid that Vasily was happy merely to let it waft in his direction. But then he realized how terribly hungry he was. How long it had been since he last ate. "Oh, Sweetums, you are such a good wife. Where is little Boris?"

"He needs a new coat, Vasilich."

"I remember you said."

"Go to his room. I wrapped him up in blankets."

Vasily stood inside Boris's room but he couldn't see little Boris anywhere. He called his name. A humongous mountain of quilts moved slightly. "Boris?" he said again. A prodigiously elevated stockpile of blankets trembled slightly. "Boris!" he yelled, exhausting his lungs. An alp of Herculean dimension wobbled slightly as if an earthquake were about to realign tectonic plates. Vasily ran to the bed in time to yank Boris from the falling promontory.

"Dad?" Boris asked. And Vasily clasped his son in a bear hug. There were tears and smiles.

Vasily had an idea. He would be able to pay the heating bill! True, for a fur collar he'd have to trap and skin a rabbit, which almost deterred him, but then, there was an endless supply of rabbits, but only one little Boris.

So Sveta taught Vasily how to thread and wield a needle, and before long, he was a master tailor. Always of coats. He sewed coats of seven colors, coats with collars and coats without, quilted coats, black coats for lawyers, wide coats for women (Russian women tended to be wide), spring jackets, and even coats for dolls.

And as he sewed, his son grew up. One day little Boris—no longer so little—announced that he wanted to be an engineer. So his father sewed some more, until he was able to send Boris to engineering school. But now the house seemed lonely.

"Sweetums," he said to Sveta, "I'm tired. I don't want to sew coats anymore."

Sweetums looked at her husband and saw that he had aged. He was still distinguished-looking, he still had that fine-boned profile, the arching nose suggestive of power, the cheekbones pointed and shiny, but there were deep valleys beneath his caramel eyes and deep gutters around his mouth. She stood on her toes to kiss him, a quick, companionable kiss.

"You've worked hard," she said, "and our son is grown up and has coats to last him a lifetime."

Vasily merely nodded. He was too tired to move his tongue and talk.

Despite his exhaustion, Sweetums thought her husband carried himself with a certain dignity and even a degree of wisdom. He was temperate and tolerant. He had sacrificed himself for his son, which is how things should go, she believed, not the son sacrificing himself for his father. She went into the kitchen for a glass and came back with a glass of vodka. "Here, Vasilich, you've earned it."

They sat on the worn-out couch in the front room while he drank the vodka.

"Sveta," he said, while she said, "Dearest."

They smiled at each other and he gestured to indicate that she should speak first.

"As I was saying," she continued, "you have worked hard and long. And you were already dead to begin with."

He nodded.

"So you worked above and beyond the call of duty."

He didn't want to brag, but it was true. He nodded again.

"Are you ready to go back to your grave?"

"I tore it up getting out, Sveta. I don't think there's any room for me now."

"Nonsense," she said. "You got out. You can get back in."

"How?" He was impressed by her ability always to find a way. But he couldn't see a way this time.

"I will ask Boris to bury you. Oh," she wept, "we will miss you, Vasilich!"

Vasily saw his wife's face flush and grow ruddy as she brushed her tears away. She too had lines on her face. She had bristles on her chin and, these latter days, complained about her knees. He saw that she would be following him before long.

Would his son do that for him? Dig a grave for him? Boris was strong and clever, a good boy, but what kid wants to dig a grave for his own father? Vasily hated the thought of putting his son through such pain.

"I'll talk with him. You'll see. It's different from the first time, when we needed you here. Boris will understand how much you long to rest in peace."

Boris did understand. He gathered shovels and hammers and two of his friends and together they built a pine coffin and dug a six-foot hole in the back yard. Vasily watched them from a bench almost as old as he was. It was a beautiful day, spring had sprung, or, rather, since spring in Russia is a weekend between winter and summer, summer had come and trees in the forests were putting out shoots, and daffodils and crocus made a great splash of color in the grasses. Somewhere, he knew, loons and grebes dived and glided on lakes and rivers and sheerwaters put in an appearance. It seemed that all the phyla were being reborn, brown bears and ducks and worms and mosses and mushrooms and bacteria and butterflies and moths and dragonflies and horse flies and black flies and everyday flies and snakes that slide unseen through tall grass or sleep in the dark beneath porch steps made of pine or birch and ospreys who enjoy showing off their skills and turtles who can upright a fellow turtle overturned and snoozing dogs and playful kittens and children jumping rope to rhymes the rest of us forget when we grow older and also the many fish who live silently underwater, maybe dreaming of dry land, where bigger fish would not eat them. He could almost see them all.

Vasily turned sideways on a bench, laid down his head, pulled up his legs, and began to snore. Boris shook his shoulder. "Dad," he said, in a tender voice, "your grave is ready."

The friends stepped aside to give father and son a moment alone.

"Be good to your mother," Vasily said. "She's an old girl and a hard taskmaster, but she knows what's best for you."

"Sure, Dad. I'll do that."

"As for you, dear boy, try to remember me without grievance."

At that, Boris's sight blurred.

Vasily climbed into the grave and the coffin, closed his eyes, and for the second time died a contented man.

MURRAY, THE SHORT-ORDER COOK

Murray, the short-order cook, found himself at the Pearly Gates on a Tuesday evening. Tuesday was always a slow day at the restaurant, but not this slow. The gates were locked, no one was checking a list or tickets, and weeds were sprouting at the base of what he took to be heaven. Or was this hell? He'd committed some sins in his day, but surely he wasn't a bad man. He showed up for work on time. He had loved his wife, who predeceased him.

Fuck, he said, immediately clapping a hand over his mouth.

He stepped gingerly off the path of righteousness to look around the side of the fence. Maybe there was another gate.

In the fenced-off field, a tall man with a white beard called to him. Murray walked over. Do you play tennis? the bearded guy asked.

A little. I'm not very good, Murray said. I'm better with a bat.

The bearded guy handed him a racket and Murray crawled under the fence.

Are you an angel? Murray asked.

God.

That's what I thought when I wound up here. Everything's so run down.

I mean I'm God.

You're— But where is St. Peter? Where are all the angels?

I let them go. God was bouncing a tennis ball with his racket.

But—but—why?

It was never a very good plan. It just didn't work out.

Murray thought of something. My wife used to say it was a hell of a way to run a railroad.

I made all those creatures, wolves and lions and bears, and then they began to eat one another. Go figure.

Well, a body's got to eat, said Murray the short-order cook.

I didn't think it through, God said, pointing his racket to indicate where Murray should stand.

Murray exchanged a few easy hits with God, then God slammed the ball to the right while Murray was on the left.

They met at the net. Forgive me, Lord, Murray said. It's not my game.

What was?

Softball. He'd belonged to a team who called themselves The Crazy Nine. A play on Crazy Eight, if not a very good one. We should have called ourselves The Old Farts, Murray said to himself.

I prefer tennis, his opponent said, because it's faster.

But you have all the time in the world!

And it weighs on me. Believe me, it's no fun. Thank God for tennis.

Murray thought sadly of his wife. He could have used a little more time with. Without thinking, he said aloud, I miss my wife.

That was a mistake too.

My wife? My wife was not a mistake!

Death. Death was a mistake. Though not even I could think of a way to keep my creatures motivated without death. Look at me. What the fuck am I doing with all the time in the world? Playing tennis.

You do seem to enjoy it. Why are the gates of heaven closed?

I'm on vacation.

You can't take a vacation!

Sure I can. I'm God.

But what about—

What about what?

What about all the people who believe in you?

Yeah, that's a problem.

You *told* them to believe in you.

Yeah, that's another problem.

Well, fix it!

How?

I'm not you. You're the one with the answers.

Sorry. As I said, I'm not.

Murray walked over to the side-court and set his racket down. I don't feel like playing tennis anymore, he said. Muttering. He didn't usually mutter but he didn't want to tick off God. He reached in his pocket and drew out a stick of gum. Minzy must not have checked out his good trousers before she left him. He'd had a habit of carrying gum in his one suit. He loved his wife but she'd gotten a little addled or scatterbrained in her old age. The funeral home should have checked his pockets too.

You don't have to play tennis. Did I say you *had* to play tennis? Murray shook his head.

I offered you an *opportunity* to play tennis. That's all. Jesus.

So you're going to open the gates?

I'm probably never going to open the gates again.

But—but—won't other people show up?

I hope not.

Are they going to hell?

There never was a hell. And now there's not a heaven.

I thought I'd see my wife again.

Oh, *that*! Okay, here's your wife.

Minzy was at his side. She had never come up to more than his shoulder and she didn't now. Murray felt a quiet joy as he looked at her. She was near-sighted and, without her glasses, the blue of her eyes was tinted with gray. Her hair, sleek and straight in the sixties, had turned curly with age. Also white. Age had filled out her figure some. She was soft and pillowy, her hair billowy.

Minzy, he said, draping an arm around her.

Oh, Murray, it's just like the Bible said! We're together again!

Was that in the Bible? Murray wondered. Of course, he'd never read the Bible. When did short-order cooks have time to read?

Minzy, this is God, Murray said.

Minzy shook God's hand. Pleased to meet you, I'm sure, she said.

Do you play tennis? God asked her.

I'm afraid not, she said, looking a bit abashed, thinking *I ought to have learned to play tennis so I could play with God. I bet he gets lonely.*

God has shut down heaven, Murray explained to her. He's on vacation.

Everybody needs a vacation now and again, said Minzy.

A *permanent* vacation, Murray said.

Oh, Minzy said, turning to God, you can't do that.

I'm sorry? God said. I can do anything I want.

No, I mean if you take a permanent vacation, how will we ever find our little daughter?

Murray was shaking his head, trying to signal to Minzy that she shouldn't bring this up.

Our little daughter, Minzy said again. She was only four when she died. Pretty and sweet and funny and full of life. Full of *life.* Minzy was weeping now, her blue eyes going grayer, tears tumbling down her face, which creased with sorrow. She tried to wipe them off with her blowzy white hair. She's supposed to be *here!* Minzy wailed.

When I closed down the operation, God said, I sent everybody to Kansas City.

Why Kansas City? asked Murray.

Why not Kansas City? You have a better idea?

No, no, Murray said quickly, Kansas City is fine. Can we get there from here?

No pro-blem-o, said God. It's just a jump, skip, and hop. The jump gets you to New York, the skip to the Mississippi River, and the hop to Kansas City.

Murray and Minzy were delighted to hear this. Their small family would be together again! Holding hands, they jumped.

Sure enough, they landed in Kansas City, and their daughter was waiting for them. In a park. Maybe a four-year-old shouldn't be alone in a park, but she was, and she didn't seem to be any the worse for it. Her moplike hair had been combed and her face and teeth were clean and shiny. The only way in which she looked a little dated was that she was wearing a pinafore. Nobody had worn pinafores for forty years, which was how long she had been dead. Minzy and Murray wept and touched, and touched and wept. "Murphy, Murphy," Murray kept saying, for he and Minzy had named her after the television character Murphy Brown, not because she was at all like the television character but because the name began with an "M," and they preferred "Murphy" to "Mary." It occurred to Murray that God might not like to hear that.

As for God? He never went back to work. Why should he, when people paid so little attention to him? He did lose interest in tennis, though, or rather, his knees gave out. He took up handicrafts, carving replicas of all the creatures he had created. This kept him busy. Occasionally he thought about Murray, whom he remembered as a pretty nice fella, polite and game.

FUGUE

I reached for the wind. It caught me up and carried me across the sky. We flew over roofs, tree tops, skyscrapers, and the Seattle Needle. My lungs were buoyant, my face, I was sure, rosy with oxygen and glee. I wished I'd brought a kite.

I suppose it's unnecessary to say it was like being in a painting by Chagall.

I flew all the way to the moon. The earth was blue, stars bright as bonfires. I think the Hubble telescope took a picture of me.

Out there I remembered my parents, both violinists, playing the Grosse Fuge. I could hear the music in my mind. And all the string quartets that included fugues.

Had I lost my sense of reason, entered a fugue? No.

But I had found a place where the cold was warm, the silence resonant, the population nil + 1. Maybe there were fossils of microbes. Did I mention the silence? It allowed me to hear the music.

The moon is 240,000 miles from the earth. It reflects the sun most of the time.

Could I ever go home? Did I want to? In ways big and small, it can be taxing to decide what one wants.

WHEN WE ARRIVED AT
THE GROCERY STORE

The shelves were overturned. Foodstuffs were rotting. Tin cans had roamed, or rolled, everywhere, like tourists. We were not tourists; we were hungry and searching. The bottled water was already gone. My husband whispered in my ear: "Grab what you can." I grabbed what I could. Outside, it was raining, hard, fast, dramatically.

DROUGHT

Water is leaving us. It's disappearing from water tanks, reservoirs, lakes and rivers. The water table is dropping. Plants are dying. The sequoias known as California redwoods, having flourished well over a millennium, are dying. In California, water is rationed. Bath water. Water for lawns. Water intended to accompany food. Jerry Brown, the governor, is not just worried; one can hear fear in his voice. His voice climbs just slightly higher when he talks about the drought in his state but the higher is enough to clue us in. What calamities will occur if the drought continues?

Will Californians continue to stay in their state? What if the forests catch on fire? But they already do. They are likely to do so again. Also likely is that at some point, as rationing increases, and water becomes more difficult to obtain barring the return of a rainy season, residents will leave for more congenial locales. Some, anyway, and no doubt later, more. Arizona, New Mexico, Nevada will not be among the places to which they move. Those who move will favor areas with sufficient precipitation. That is bound to mean the North, with its snow and rain. It's true that there are storms in the South but there are also hurricanes and tornadoes in the South, and people looking to escape from one disaster won't want to have to deal with another.

Animals also head north but thousands of them die along the way, especially the pets who were abandoned when people fled. The dogs and cats, especially the small ones, the turtles and the goldfish will not make it to the Far North. (The goldfish will be turned out of their fishbowls without ceremony, and before any of the goldfish realize what is happening.)

So the people move north and the population of Northern cities multiplies. People are crowding one another. There's not enough room to breathe. Some people are angry about this. They buy guns or get out the guns they already have. Road rage is rampant. The homeless, packed in parks, sleep folded up in lobbies and thresholds and raid garbage cans for food but there is never enough food for all the homeless. Some jump fences, racing to flag outgoing planes but airline workers shove them back. Some ride boxcars, and a few of them make it to Anchorage or Fairbanks.

When they get there, they discover that Russians and Japanese are there, too. They will have come over the Bering Strait. They will wear shorts and tee-shirts. Snowpacks are melting. Snow is melting. Igloos are melting—and the Inuit designed them never to melt. To the Russians and the Japanese, it seems as if they themselves are melting.

South Americans, on the other hand, have followed the Andes mountains to the Drake Passage, hoping to get to Antarctica. But we will stick to what most concerns us.

All over the world, people head for the mountains. From the worn-out Appalachians to the Himalayans of Uttarakhand to the Kamchatka Peninsula. It does no good. Once, mountaintops were cooled by crosswinds, and people and animals were invigorated, refreshed; now the hot tongues of sunshine flick and lick until people and animals are fatigued, too fatigued to climb farther, and they look in vain for even an inch of shade before they crawl behind a boulder to die.

The constant sun enervates. Yes, night still arrives, but one's skin is burnt so bad that sores appear on arms, legs, and bald heads. People give up on clothes, abandon their garments, for it is too painful to wear them. Everyone gives up.

Which makes everyone else want to give up. And why not? Humans cannot live without water. Yes, there have been attempts to desalinate seawater. And some have worked. Briefly. Recycled wastewater is also promising. The problem is, neither works well enough to produce the quantities of fresh water that we need at the rate at which we need it.

Which is why these days you (who *are* you?) will find us dying, always in places that used to promise water. Just before we die, we often hallucinate. Images of waterfalls, running rivers, water fountains, and rain rain rain leave our tongues hanging out, our eyes popping, our throats dry as martinis or deserts. Dry as calcification. Dry as a ponderous pedagogue. Dry as a basement of vampires with no fresh throats to suck.

We hankered for salt. Could anything be more ironic?

Renal failure was common. It led to cardiac problems.

We were too exhausted to lick our own lips.

AEGEA

Eight hundred years: that's how long it took to design and develop the space ark. It would hold a thousand people, chosen by lottery. Some thought we should have bred a generation of geniuses specifically for this purpose, but others of us felt that was rather Fascistic. Surprisingly, most older people—and the majority demographic was old—did not want to go. They preferred to die with Earth. It was home, after all. Of course, they also wanted us to take their children and grandchildren but we had to stick to the rules of the lottery. Thank goodness children were allowed to enter the lottery at the age of ten; the trip would have been heartbreaking without them. They kept our spirits up, those kids.

Those of us who boarded the ark would later wonder if we had made the right choice.

We located our destination some decades in advance. Climate and geography seemed manageable, earthlike seasons existed, water and air were abundant. Were there aliens on Aegea? (Somewhere along the line someone had come up with that name and it stuck, presumably because of its bountiful bodies of water.) That, of course, was a secondary question, considering our situation.

The space ark ran on dark energy. Literally, as we had set the ark on a path of dark energy, which meant we could travel at ninety percent of the speed of light (we whipped through the geosynchronous orbits in about a second and a half, or so it seemed). Also, we had evolved from human to robohuman, and that made some things easier for us. Our knees did not wear out. Internal computers kept tabs on and sustained our hearts. 3-D printouts could fix almost anything, including our internal computers.

There were, as it turned out, aliens. They surrounded the ark. They were remarkably tall (ten feet? nine and a half?), broad-shouldered, with dark rings around their eyes, like raccoons. Bandit eyes, we say about raccoons. The rings were not from lack of sleep. They were not masks, not face paint. Actual fur.

If we played basketball with them, we would, obviously, lose.

They were not interested in basketball. They were more interested in eating us. They carried spears almost as long as they were.

We had not been so foolish as not to bring weapons of our own, though we'd hoped any aliens would be friendly. We had no idea how many they were, whether there were aliens elsewhere on Aegea, whether all the aliens on Aegea wielded spears, whether there were tribes or nations and, if so, whether some of them would grasp our plight and come to our rescue. Our weapons back home included nuclear warheads and long-range missiles, but we had come here to live, not to die as a result of our own drastic technology.

An Aegean even taller than the others stabbed his spearpoint into the ground, indicating that he wished to talk. We let down the steps and opened the door to the ark.

What came out of his mouth was a sound like a radio playing in the distance, yet every one of us could hear it. Or maybe it was more like the plaint of a mourning dove. Or the call of a loon. In fact, it seemed to be all of those things, and also like the hum of a hummingbird's wings, or the singing dog of New Guinea.

What it was not was angry, ferocious, bloodlustful. So why the spears? And why were they licking their lips? Yes, they had lips.

And yet the melancholy music that issued from his throat suggested the alien was closer to death than we were. There was a vague hint of a rattle in his throat, and we knew he needed help. Maybe the other aliens didn't—we couldn't hear them from where they were—but we knew this particular alien was close to death. Could we help him? The ship's captain did not step outside the ark but waited for the sick alien to negotiate the flight stairs. Several of us got up from our seats so he could lie down on them. There were three seats in each row, and his legs stretched across the aisle onto a fourth. There were several doctors on board to examine the creature.

Their examination took a while. We figured they were, in a way, trying to translate his body into our language. A breakthrough came when they determined that his voice, so various and complex, was not only *his* voice: it was the voice of *all* the aliens. Each alien was linked to every other alien, sort of as if there were a network of aliens, interconnected and integrated. Then we thought, *Are the other aliens also dying?* We looked outside again. And they were. They were dying. And they'd sunk all the spears into the ground, like the first one. They had never thought to kill and eat us; they came to us for help.

We wanted to help them. Of course we did.

Though we also wanted to find out what was destroying them in case it tried to destroy us.

The diagnosis our doctors developed? That the aliens were dying of thirst.

How could that be, with all the water on Aegea? Well, of course much of that water was salt water. But that wasn't the only reason, though it explained why the aliens were licking their lips.

Something else had got into the water. A slimy little bacterium in the shape of a rod.

Did we bring antibiotics? You bet we brought antibiotics!

No way we would we not have brought antibiotics!

The doctors tested various antibiotics on our dying alien, who grew paler and thinner at first, his bandit eyes taking up most of his face, but when the doctors injected him with linezolid the rattle stopped and some color came back. (He was not green, he'd never been green; his skin was like ours, a light brown, and presumably the aliens didn't have to shave and didn't grow fur on their chins, but we didn't know for sure.) We knew he was improving.

A few hours later—it was now night, a night like the inside of a black boot buried in a deep cave, a night too dark to allow for a single step unless one already knew the way, which we did not—he was able to sit up. We wondered if the aliens outside the ark were also able to sit up, but we had to wait till daylight to find out.

They were indeed sitting up, all of them. A contingent came to the bottom of the steps to the ark. Our captain opened the door. They thanked us. The alien still lying across the aisle told us that. He stood, or tried to, but he was forced to stoop slightly. Then we saw the most wonderful thing: he smiled. We smiled back. All the aliens outside the ship smiled.

It is a glorious thing to find friends in a foreign place, a foreign planet. We had not expected that. Soon the aliens—they called themselves a name we translated as "born-here"—offered to show us around. Not all at once; two aliens would take ten people to a cavern, a lake, a city. We went to museums, churches, schools and universities. They took us shopping. They told us some of their history.

They had always been interconnected, they told us. They had always shared their thoughts with one another. Nothing was hidden, nothing mysterious. At first we found this marvelous: no one held subversive opinions or dangerous desires; no one could plan a mass shooting without everybody else knowing about it. Crime stopped before it began. As we listened to them, we remembered our own history on earth with profound sadness.

On the ark, flight attendants handed out meals. Through the windows we could see sunlight melting into the colors of fruit: citron, blueberry, peach, orange, raspberry, cherry, and plum. Then we became aware that all of us were observing the same thing. The same colors. The same melting.

It was as if we were melting into one another.

We sat up straight. We were alert. We were frightened.

Just as there could be no individuality among the aliens, there would no longer be anyone among us who would write a transcendent symphony, paint a surprising painting, sculpt the remarkable sculpture, sing a song as beautiful as Schubert's songs, write a poem or book that would change hearts and minds.

We stared straight ahead, not looking at one another, because if we did we would be ashamed. And we would see that shame reflected on every face. Hadn't we thought we were unique? Hadn't we thought that even if we ourselves were nothing special there were those who were and they would compensate for our failures? Hadn't we believed in greatness, in originality, in authenticity? In what was discrete and distinctive? Now—

We were, to say the least, disheartened. Maybe we would adapt to new measures, but it wouldn't be easy. It was definitely not going to be easy.

THE END OF TIME

. . . is the end of motion. Everything, every life stops. Insects cease to crawl, fly, weave or bore, cease (an unanticipated benefit) to bite, sting, suck. The panther ceases to prowl, the rooster to crow. The Ruddy Turnstone ceases to strut his stuff on the railing of the pier (he who had looked as though he were about to moonwalk or breakdance). A field mouse ceases to gnaw, her tail to twitch. The pretty aspen, Sally Rand among trees, a divorced mom with a kid to support and no high school diploma so there was never exactly a whole bunch of job opportunities, stops flashing her fans, folds her leaves and falls still. A rusted tin man was never stiller than she.

Water stops running. Wind stops blowing. Rain stops falling, and the droplets are like a net suspended in midair.

Nothing is going on.

Nothing is doing, nothing worth talking about. There will be no gossip ever again, because there will never be anything again to gossip about.

And the only news will be way too old and exhausted to call news.

Light from supernovae that exploded millions of years ago, or just yesterday (it's all the same, yesterday and yesterday and yesterday), will have long since arrived on earth and left, leaving the sky dark even in daytime.

As you see, the sun's stopped shining, the seasons have stopped turning. The earth, Galileo, does not move now.

Traffic jams. Airplanes hang in the sky as if drawn there, brushstroke birds in a Chinese painting. Hydraulic plants shut down. Workers quit.

Everywhere, a computer crashes.

The silence is as huge as a secret.

Verbs have ceased to exist altogether. Even forms of to be imply some equation of equivalence, some easy back and forth, give and take, an interaction or the possibility of interaction. Nor can language move anyone now: Perhaps it can be contemplated, admired, reflected upon, perhaps worshiped—but loved? Can anyone love a syntax whose perfection is as stationary as an exercise bike? an exercise bike bolted to the floor? an exercise bike bolted to the floor of a house owned by a quadriplegic?

It is a sad day, this last day no night follows. Sad down to the complete inside of things.

The molecules, which have always from the very beginning of time loved to dance, stop their softshoe-shuffling, their toe-tapping, even their finger-snapping-in-time-to-the-music. They stop bowing and curtseying, stop fox-trotting and tangoing, stop putting the right foot in and taking the right foot out and putting the right foot in again and this time shaking it all about, stop doing the Charleston, the jitterbug, the twist, the fish, the monkey, disco nights, the Macarena. The new song of atomic anomie goes,

No more bump. No more grind.

No more matter. No more mind.

It is a sad day when little dogs sniffing the grass in low-lying coastal areas are swept out to sea.

It is a sad day when a heart stops between beats.

A sad day, when the Black Lab forgets to lick her arthritic paws in front of the fire.

But babies cease crying. Another benefit!

But lovers quit arguing and apologizing, parents cease helping with homework or glancing at the front door and wondering when the hell Bekki, formerly Becky, is going to come home tonight. Policemen cease policing, scholars turn their backs on footnotes. A woman puts down her book, which has ceased telling its story anyway (*I'm Not Stiller*, by Max Frisch). A favorite ballpoint pen—which had come in the mail to her home from the Doris Day Animal League ("Write" a "wrong" against animals, it reminded the charitable contributor) but which she had used for the first time while paying for a purchase in Sturgeon Bay, Wisconsin, when, reaching rummagingly into her purse, she happened upon it, felt its comfortably narrow circumference and knew it would become a favorite—approaching a predicate in mid-sentence (in the hotel room was a Jacuzzi, and not knowing any better she and her husband—foolishly, the two lovers imagined they would marry and already called each other husband, wife—had poured in so much bubble stuff that the water jets churned up an avalanche of bubbles, bubbles as swirly-thick as meringue, bubbles so stiff and soapy as to create an iridescent curtain that stood straight up in the air in a sort of canopy, and when they got into bed, under the old-fashioned white lace coverlet, their skin was as soft and slick and sensitive to each other as an internal organ, and his hand between her legs was as hot and searing as a brand), and finding, instead of a verb, a void, a linguistic bridge washed out by flash floods, by the end of copulation, everything unhitched and remaining unhitched, plummets helplessly into the unspannable, untraversable lacuna between nouns and vanishes, the way all favorite ballpoints eventually disappear forever, lost behind sofa pillows or between pages of a book someone had expected to underline but then closed and put back on a shelf and forgot.

DEFINING THE INDEFINABLE

"Not infrequently" is slightly fewer than "fairly often."

TERMINATION EQUATIONS

Termination equations bisected the blackboard. And everything else. "Doomsday has—" *arrived*, Professor Banks was going to say, but there was no longer a Professor Banks. There was no longer a blackboard. There were no longer any students. The bubble created by the Higgs Boson, tunneling toward earth, had risen to the surface and popped. Was the whole universe gone? But there was no one to ask that question, much less anyone to answer it.

If the people were gone, were there still buildings in the city? Skyscrapers? Did small dogs still yap, kittens purr? Did horses still taste the sweet grass, and did cattle still give milk? Did a three-year-old anywhere ride a tricycle?

Did the sun still shine or rain fall?

But these are rhetorical questions, with which the good professor would not have bothered himself.

Let us ask instead if Doomsday might be followed by rebirth. Yes, on the surface, it seems unlikely, but surfaces often conceal layers.

But no, if there are no surfaces, and clearly the bubble has left none, there are no layers. There is no way out of this nothingness, nor will any God come to our rescue.

So what can we do?

Can we feed the caged birds?

Can we pack lunches for our children?

Can we listen to music?

Can we write poems?

But no, we cannot feed the birds, pack lunches for our children, listen to music, or write poems. We no longer exist. Not only are there no affirmative answers, there are no questions. This page does not exist. You say it does? Hold it to a mirror.

No reflection. A digital delusion.

The universe has swallowed itself, the snake its tail.

WHAT WE FOUND WHEN WE ARRIVED AT THE END

Nothing dark, nothing dangerous. Just more of the same. Yet it was not the same, if only because it occurred later. Cement pavement, graded streets, traffic lights, trees trimmed to allow for telephone wires. I hated that. To my husband, I said, "Kiss me." He did. A breeze got caught in my hair.

AWAITING THE APOCALYPSE

As the Apocalypse approached, we lounged around the house like Romans of yore, nibbling black olives and Brie, perhaps a prune or grapes. We had run out of things to say, because no one had anything to say in the face of an apocalypse. We might have said "I love you" but that was so abstract. Nibbling was realer, if we can say that one thing is more real than another and we certainly can.

We had discussed an orgy but hadn't the energy for it. That was too great a leap into reality, considering that we would soon be nothing at all. We would no longer be men or women, parents or grandparents or godfathers, or students or accountants or grocery store checkers-out. And that was just the beginning. Not only the lights but the sky would go out. The earth would be pulled out from under us like a much-used carpet. Birds would fly away but then fall because there would be no air there for them to breathe. Naturally, lassitude consumed us. Death is death, and at some point it makes no sense to struggle any longer. Even nibbling became arduous. Who wants to eat grapes while dying? Black olives are lovely, but they are no defense against the end.

Still, something had to be done. The combo of anxiety and boredom was wrecking us. We felt sick, frustrated, frightened. Could we play chess? No. Could we guess at movie titles? No.

Nor could we watch reruns of "Friends." The Friends were now middle-aged and waiting for the Apocalypse just as we were.

All in all, it was a very bad situation. I whispered into my husband's ear. What I said was "We have to do something."

"No, we don't," he said. "All we have to do is wait and something will be done."

"Nobody's having any fun."

"Nor should they," he said.

"Oh but they should! It's our last chance."

"Our last dance?"

"Last *chance*!"

"But there isn't any chance at all, Poo Pie," he said. He often called me that. I liked to think it was an endearment. Maybe it was. Or maybe he thought I was a simpleton. That could be true too. "Last chance for what?" he asked.

I mumbled something. I said, "Last chance as in last chance to gas up before we hit the desert."

"You must have noticed we are not anywhere near a desert."

"It's a metaphor. You know what a metaphor is."

"I do. But probably they shouldn't be used so freely. Metaphors can be misleading."

I was feeling tireder than ever. A married couple can do that to each other.

"Don't blame me," he said. "I'm just lying here calmly, waiting to welcome the Apocalypse."

Although we were on the bed, we were not in pajamas. He had shorn off his hair and now vaguely resembled Bruce Willis, and he wore denims and a tee-shirt but no shoes. I was pretty much his mirror image, except I had hair and hoped to keep it, but not everybody gets to. Age. Age was a factor here. Maybe we would not have been so quiescent had we been younger.

"I believe you are right about that," he said. "If we were younger, we might be mounting a revolution. Riding shotgun. Tearing down the old to make room for the new."

"We can do that now," I said.

"We cannot. If we tore down the old, there would still be no new to arise." This time his voice curled under his tongue for a moment, expressing his own distaste for our predicament.

"Has the President Tweeted us yet?"

"Nope. And why would he? He knows nothing can be done."

"He could at least say he's sorry."

"It's not his fault."

"But he must know *something*. What about the CIA? The FBI? The Secretary of State?"

"None of them know anything."

"Scientists," I said. "Scientists always know something."

"A few of them do. The rest are arguing about meteorites and climate change. They are every bit as confused as we are."

"How long do you think we have to wait?"

"Nobody knows."

"But if nobody knows, maybe there's time to do something! Even if it's only time to have fun."

"Poo Pie, there's no reason to have fun, because the end is before us."

"Not yet."

"Maybe. Maybe not."

"Does fun have to have a reason? Doesn't the very fact of fun having a reason take the fun out of it?"

"You are so stubborn," he said, tousling my hair.

"So are you."

"Hmpf," he said.

And at that we drifted into a silence that neither of us could deflect. Despite all the nibbling I'd done, I was growing hungry. Maybe for a steak. I hated to eat meat because it causes so much suffering, but the animals were all going to die with us. They weren't going to outlive us. Maybe that's a piss poor reason for falling away from vegetarianism, but it was a reason. Besides, I hated vegetables, which meant I was in a real double bind. I wound up eating a lamb chop, but I was annoyed with myself afterward. Why do people always do things, then second-guess themselves, then third-guess themselves, then reach for the Balvenie. That's what I did. And the Apocalypse had still not happened.

Then my husband opened a pack of cigarettes. He had quit a few years ago. I'd asked him to. "I'm going to die first," I'd said, because I'm a little older than he is, "and I need you to be around to take care of me when that happens."

Now he was breaking his promise.

"Promises no longer matter," he said. "We're going to go out together. POO PIE," he said, leaning on his nickname for me until it sounded as loud as a bomb, "no one's going to read our living wills! No one's going to receive our legacies. There will be no doctors to take our vitals. There will be no banks to hold our money."

"Such as it is," I grumbled. It wasn't much.

"Unlike that weird TV show, there will be nobody *left behind.*"

I knew he was telling the truth. I knew also that there was no particular point in telling the truth. Telling the truth was a waste of time. As, of course, was everything else.

"You have to face up to this," he said.

"I know. I'm trying. I am."

We heard a sound. As if wood were cracking.

We went to the window. A tree fell into the pond. It made a splash. A literal splash. Then the floor beneath us began to shake. So we were shaking too. Windows cracked and shards winged off, or at us. We stumbled into each other's arms. We looked up at the ceiling. Was there time to run out? We ran out. The air was burnt. Logs were on fire—outside, not inside the house. The moon went out as if had been a wired connection. We heard crying, barking, cats hissing, animals stampeding, but none of this lasted long enough for contemplation. Holding hands was complicated; in fact, terribly difficult. Stuff flying around kept separating us. Maybe the secret was to shut our eyes. Maybe if we shut our eyes none of this would be happening. We gave each other a last look and then shut our eyes. Shut our eyes. Shut our eyes.

THE QUIET END

It comes after the sun expands and vaporizes the earth. The universe will backshift, reverse, relapse into a simpler situation, the cosmos dead-dark. Nothing in it will be capable of creating anything. There is no source of energy anywhere. How long does this last? Presumably, forever. Does that mean the cosmos is a corpse? But corpses degrade. (They rot.) Will there be a residue, like, say, ashes? Or will there be nothing, as there was nothing before there was something? Our languages are not adequate to talk about this. How are we to define nothingness? There are words, but the words are meaningless synonyms. We cannot see, hear, touch, taste, or smell nothingness. To say it is the absence of something, or all and every possible somethings, is to say, precisely, nothing. Say a leaf falls into a vacuum. The leaf is something. Is the vacuum something? Maybe. Maybe not. It depends, perhaps, on how we define a vacuum. Let's define it as a space in which nothing exists. So is nothingness now a something? It's useful to remember that by the time this question becomes pertinent we will be long gone.

ONCE UPON A TIME

Once upon a time, there was no time, or rather, time was more like a space: a crib, a parent's arms, the blank air filling with the transcendent sounds of your mother and father playing their violins. At some point, time broke in half: play time and sleepy time, and eventually they became day time and night time. A single day could last a decade. You had no idea how long night time was because you slept through it, although dangerous dreams raised your anxiety, or maybe your anxiety raised dangerous dreams. You cried when your mother enrolled you in some kind of play center. You were supposed to make a potholder. The last thing you wanted to do was make a potholder. You didn't understand that your mother just wanted a little time and space of her own. She worked tirelessly, you thought, not understanding how hard she worked and how tired she was. Then school intervened, and that was a good thing. You were an angry child, a child who felt she had to fend for herself, muscle her way into the world, and at the same time a child too shy to do that, which meant interacting with others was awkward, which meant you were sent to the principal's office again and again. But books were a blessing; learning was a blessing. You made up homework for yourself, for the fun of it. You enrolled your little sister and a Down's Syndrome kid from next door in your private school, where you were the teacher and assigned homework. In fifth grade, the teacher called on you while you were reading *The Black Stallion*.

Time passed before you realized you were being addressed. The entire class laughed. Fortunately, the teacher laughed too, and you returned to your reading and nobody made you stop.

But starting with the sixth grade, time speeded up. There were friends and enemies. You fell in love with a boy in third grade who gave a piano concert in the school auditorium. He was Polish. How he got to Richmond, Virginia, you never found out, but he played the piano far better than you did, and you were older. The lesson was not lost on you and two years later you quit the piano. Of course, you never told anyone you loved a younger man. And the year after that you fell in love with the class clown. What you loved about him was that he was a cut-up. Nobody knew you were in love. Certainly not him.

Love eats up so much energy. At least the love that is unknown, untold, hidden behind dreams does so. Sometimes I look around me at all the people and try to figure out which of them are in love without anybody knowing about it.

Enough about love. Next came sex, which complicates the situation whatever the situation may be. "The Male Gaze," as they say, the Tango with its composing and opposing postures. The male bullying, the belligerence, the masculine assumption of rights. All true, but how does a woman protect herself when, after all, she, too, is sexual?

Freedom from hormones is not insignificant. One can think better without them. One is more at peace, if not actually at peace. And there is still time to do something. A little something, at least.

I think so.

Maybe.

Yet some time has been lost. Or not just some. A lot. A lot of time has been lost.

Who would have thought?

Who would have ever thought?

The thing is, there's not much left. At least, not relative to what there was.

We must do something about this. Maybe we can dig through the past and save a few scraps of time and piece them together to make time longer. Rummaging through salvage may turn up some decay and dread, but possibly also a few memories in which we can lose ourselves, daydreaming and pondering. Preferably on a warm day on a sheet on the grass while your husband pours lemonade into your glass and gold finches flutter on a branch.

On such a day, butterflies light on flowering bushes and the dog rolls over on his back to soak in the sun. On such a day, a tender breeze salves one's skin.

Seize the day, we say and say and say, and it is true that this is what remains. A single day. Which must be seized if it is not to be lost. How lovely the transient, how admirable the souls passing through, how content the butterflies and the sleeping dog.

Kelly Cherry was the Poet Laureate of Virginia, 2010 –2012, and is the author of twenty-six books, ten chapbooks, and two translations of classical drama. Her most recent book is *Quartet for J. Robert Oppenheimer* (poetry), and forthcoming is *Weather*, a chapbook, and *Beholder's Eye*, a new full-length book of poems. She is an Emeritus Member of Poets Corner at the Cathedral Church of St. John the Divine in New York City, and was the first recipient of the Hanes Poetry Prize from the Fellowship of Southern Writers. Her many other awards include fellowships from the National Endowment for the Arts and the Rockefeller Foundation, a Bradley Achievement Award, the William "Singing Billy" Walker Award for Lifetime Achievement in Southern Letters, the L.E. Phillabaum Poetry Award, the Carole Weinstein Prize in Poetry, and a USIS Speaker Award (the Philippines). She is the Eudora Welty Professor Emerita of English and Evjue-Bascom Professor Emerita in the Humanities, University of Wisconsin Madison, and a University of Alabama in Huntsville Eminent Scholar, 2001-2005. She and her husband live on a farm in Virginia.